STORIES OF GLITTER, THE KINGDOM IN THE CAVERNS

A DRAGON LORDS OF VALDIER ANTHOLOGY

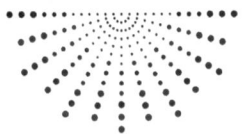

S. E. SMITH

MONTANA
PUBLISHING

ACKNOWLEDGMENTS

I would like to thank my husband Steve for believing in me and being proud enough of me to give me the courage to follow my dream. I would also like to give a special thank you to my sister and best friend, Linda, who not only encouraged me to write, but who also read the manuscript. Also to my other friends who believe in me: Julie, Jackie, Christel, Sally, Jolanda, Lisa, Laurelle, Debbie, and Narelle. The girls that keep me going!

And a special thanks to Paul Heitsch, David Brenin, Samantha Cook, Suzanne Elise Freeman, and PJ Ochlan—the awesome voices behind my audiobooks!

—S.E. Smith

CONTENTS

FOR THE LOVE OF TIA

THE DRAGONLINGS AND THE
MAGIC FOUR-LEAF CLOVER

THE KING'S QUEST

FOR THE LOVE OF TIA

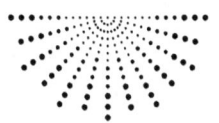

SYNOPSIS

Tia is the Keeper of the Stories for the inhabitants of Glitter. She dreams of a life she knows will never happen, but hope blossoms when a strange creature is captured at the entrance to their kingdom, and Tia remembers the legend of the goddess that will renew their world.

Jett's thirst for adventure leads him to a previously undiscovered cavern where an unusual kingdom exists, and he is captivated by their beautiful Keeper. Unable to resist, he returns again and again until he knows he must steal her away.

CHAPTER ONE

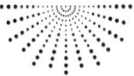

ia sighed as she ran her delicate fingers over the smooth surface of the scroll. Her eyes stared blankly at the intricate illustrations and the symbols carefully describing each legend. Her tiny, light green ears flickered back and forth at the sound of rapidly approaching footsteps drawing her out of her trance. She knew immediately who it was – her brother Tamblin.

She quickly rolled the scroll and hid it behind one of the colorful fabric tapestries she had hanging in her room. She didn't want him to know that she had been writing down the stories of their people, at least not yet. He would be deeply concerned if he knew and become even more protective of her.

Tia closed her large brown eyes and drew in a deep breath in an effort to calm the fast beat of her heart. Every third beat, it would stop and she was terrified it would not start again. It was happening more often and lasting longer each time. She opened her eyes and forced a smile onto her face as her brother swept aside the long curtain door of her chambers.

"Tia, I have need of you," Tamblin said in his deep, rich voice. "A creature has been captured at the entrance to our caverns. It is very large and strange-looking."

Tia tilted her head and frowned. "Why do you need me? Surely you do not expect me to give you my permission to kill it?" she asked scornfully. "You have never bothered to ask me before!" she pointed out, reminding him of the few times when an unknown creature wandered into their domain only to be killed within moments by the Guardians of the Cavern, two large WereBeast with poisonous saliva and barb-like fur.

Tamblin glared at her before straightening his broad shoulders. Even though he stood no taller than twelve inches tall, he was still taller than most of the other inhabitants of Glitter. As their ruler, he guarded the kingdom and its populaces with a fierce protectiveness that Tia knew she should appreciate more. A soft sigh escaped her. With her, he tended to be three times more protective, rarely letting her travel anywhere alone.

"Tia," he said, drawing in a deep breath to calm his frustration. "This creature is different from anything I have ever encountered before. The Guardians alerted us and we were able to render it unconscious before they attacked and killed it. As Keeper of the Stories, I thought it would be wise to seek your counsel first before I ordered it destroyed." He paused a moment and his eyes softened as he studied her. "I do respect your guidance, sister."

Tia lowered her eyes and blinked several times, ashamed of her unreasonable criticism. "I will come. Where is the creature now?"

"I have had it transported to the center of the moss field, near the river," Tamblin said, gently wrapping his hand around her arm. He frowned down at her in concern. "You have lost more weight. Have you not been feeling well again?"

Tia bit her lower lip with her sharp teeth and shook her head. "I'm fine, Tamblin. You have more important things to worry about than me," she assured him.

"Never, Tia," Tamblin responded quietly, guiding her out to the flying creatures they used as transport throughout the caverns. "You will always be the most important thing to me."

He helped her climb up onto the saddle that was strapped on the back of one of the bat-like creatures that lived in the caverns. Tia leaned forward and petted the body of the flying mammal that was covered in a thick, dark gray fur with large, black leathery wings. The winged animal turned and emitted a low humming noise when it saw Tia, its sharp pointed ears flicking back and forth in affection. Tamblin adjusted the tiny bridle and checked Tia's saddle to make sure she was comfortable.

"Tamblin," Tia said, leaning forward to touch her brother's shoulder before he moved away. She waited until he looked at her before she smiled. "Thank you."

"I love you, Tia," Tamblin said quietly. "I only want to keep you safe."

"I know," she responded lightly. "I know. Now, let us see what marvelous creature you have discovered."

Tia snapped the reins on her flying beast and drew in a shaky breath as it rose swiftly into the air. She loved flying. She loved the freedom. Sometimes when she had trouble breathing, she would close her eyes and imagine she was as free as the flying beasts were. It helped to calm the panic that rose inside her.

"Jett," a soft whispered voice called out frantically. "You are going to get not only yourself killed but me too!"

Jett turned and grinned at the dark sand-colored face rushing up behind him. "Santil, if you are afraid of death, go back. I want to see the underground world again," he said with a silent laugh before turning to scoot through the narrow opening between the dark rocks.

"You want to see the female again, you mean," Santil growled out. "Did you not see the huge creatures that just flew into the cave? They could step on us and not even know it. We will be nothing but a pile of goo on the bottom of their feet."

Jett just shook his head. Santil was always looking at the gloomy side of things. Jett was the youngest son of the King of the Sand Kingdom. His thirst for adventure had gotten him into trouble more than once, but he loved the freedom of soaring over the sands, even if it meant being in danger of being eaten every once in a while.

Several months back, he and Santil had been flying over the sand dunes scouting for enemy worms that had attacked one of their military posts on the outer rim of their Kingdom. A small pod of the damn things had surprised them. Santil had been thrown off of his sand skimmer. Jett had engaged the worms and led them away. Unfortunately, he had encountered a large pod of them and was forced to seek shelter. That was how he found the small crack in the rocks that had led down to the most incredible kingdom under the sands.

And that is where I found my bride, he thought with satisfaction. *Now all I have to do is steal her away.*

Jett jumped down off the high rock face, landing on the smooth surface. He knew the tunnel by heart now. He had returned to it over and over since he discovered it, watching, waiting, wanting.

The first time he saw the delicate, green female he had been entranced by her beauty. Her large, dark brown eyes spoke of secrets he wanted to know. She moved like the sands dancing in the wind, barely touching the surface.

She always wore a gown that was made of the colors of the sky before a storm. His fingers itched to peel it from her slender figure. He wanted to run his lips around her tiny pointed ears and see if his whispered words of love would be returned.

He had no doubt in his mind that he loved her. She was with him every single moment whether he was awake or asleep. His mind could picture every small smile she gave to one of the many people of her clan that came to see her.

He loved to watch her as she studied the plants and mushroom shaped trees of her underground world. But he also worried that she would not care for the bright world of his kingdom. He feared she would not enjoy the sands or the fierce winds and storms that sometimes swept over his home.

"Well, are we going or are you going to stand there daydreaming all day?" Santil asked in irritation, jumping down to stand next to him.

Jett started when he realized that he had been dreaming instead of walking. He turned to look at Santil for a moment before turning his head to look down the dark tunnel. Making up his mind, he turned back to his friend once more.

"I want you to stay here," Jett commanded. "I will return in a few hours and when I do, I won't be alone. I plan to bring my bride with me."

Santil rolled his eyes in exasperation. "Don't you think you should ask her if she is interested in you first before you steal her away?"

Jett grinned at his friend. "What fun is there in that? Besides, what if she were to say no?"

Santil watched as his childhood friend sprinted down the dark tunnel, shaking his head in resignation. "How could she say no? No one ever has to you. Besides even if she did, you wouldn't listen." He chuckled as he talked to himself before jumping back up onto the ledge and leaning back against the rocky side so he could stare out at the bright sky waiting patiently for his friend to return.

CHAPTER TWO

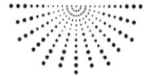

ia stared in disbelief at the unconscious figure lying on the dark red moss. The stories flowed through her mind in vivid detail. She would never forget them. They were a part of her.

The legends spoke of a beautiful goddess with hair the color of white gold that would return life to their world. Several generations ago, giants from a distant world came in great ships and took the small creatures that fed on the minerals in the sand. The creatures, in return, had left their excreta that fertilized the planet, causing the growth of the huge mushroom forests.

When the last of the creatures were taken, their world began to die as there was nothing to fertilize the seeds buried deep within the sands. The vast forests of mushroom trees withered and died. The great storms that frequently developed grew worse because there were no forests to buffer their winds.

Soon, the sand began swallowing everything. What was worse was the giants had brought with them great worms that attacked Tia's people, killing most of her clan. Their only hope of salvation was to seek the protective walls of the rock caverns.

Over the last ten generations, they had developed their world until it was the beautiful kingdom that lay before her. Her body trembled as her heart jerked uncomfortably in her chest. Her last wish had been to see her people free to go to the surface, but she never believed that it would happen in her lifetime. Now, she knew that the gods had heard her desperate plea and were giving her this last gift before she died.

"What do you think, Tia," Tamblin asked quietly as he studied the still figure lying on the moss. "Should I order it destroyed?"

"NO!" Tia cried out, looking at him in horror before remembering he did not have the knowledge that she did, at least not yet. "No," she said in a quieter voice. "She has been sent by the gods and goddesses. She is the one. She has the knowledge to heal our world above so that we may live once more in the brightness."

Tamblin looked at Tia in disbelief before turning his head to look down at the figure that was now beginning to stir. He raised his hand in a silent command for his soldiers to be ready for anything. He would order the sharp spears, laced with the poison of the Guardians of the Cavern, to strike if the creature tried to attack.

How could the Gods or Goddesses send such a large creature as their salvation? He had listened to the stories his mother had told Tia when she didn't think he was listening. He could not see the stories in his head like his sister could, but he knew they were important.

Tamblin pushed Tia behind him when the creature slowly sat up. It was obvious the creature was female. She had many of the same features as their females did.

He watched suspiciously as she blinked several times before she glanced around her. His soldiers had taken to the air and were making careful sweeps around her, keeping just far enough away to stay out of her reach but close enough that they could launch the spears if need be. He straightened to his full height, refusing to cower in fear.

"Hello," the golden goddess said with a soft smile as her gaze settled on him and his sister.

Tia stepped nimbly around Tamblin to get a closer look at the giant female, but stopped at the husky sound of her voice. Tamblin moved swiftly next to Tia, scolding her to stay behind him. Tia ignored her brother. She knew deep down that the golden creature wouldn't hurt her.

"She will not harm me," she hissed out to her brother. "She is the one! I know it." She could see the images in her head of the golden goddess her mother told her would come to save their world.

Tamblin fought the urge to bundle his sister back up onto the flying beast and lock her away in the palace where he knew she was safe. He knew she was sick even as she tried to hide it from him. He could see the tremor in her hands, the weight she had lost, and how she had trouble breathing at times. He feared if she got too excited it might bring on an attack. He glanced worriedly from Tia's face to the creature who was sitting quietly waiting for them to respond to her.

Tamblin reluctantly nodded his head. He knew deep down that this was something he could not deny his sister. The golden goddess kept her hands on her thighs and waited as Tia slowly approached her. Tia tilted her head again, her ears twitching to and fro when the creature spoke again. She might not understand her words but she did recognize the gentle tone.

Tia stepped cautiously closer, reaching out and touching the larger female with the tips of her long green fingers. She smiled when the creature remained still. Feeling more confident, she moved a little closer.

Her heart pounded erratically when the female slowly raised one of her arms. She froze in fear, wondering if she could have been mistaken. As much as she was confident that this was the creature the stories told of, she was still unprepared for the size of it. Tia watched as the female slowly lowered one of her hands down onto the soft moss, palm upward. Tia looked back and forth between the palm and the creature's eyes before making the decision to trust her instincts.

She took a tentative step forward, stopping when Tamblin hissed out again in alarm. Shaking her head at him, she climbed up into the open palm. She couldn't resist running her slender fingers over the warm flesh of the creature.

It was soft and smooth – almost comforting. Tia glanced up and watched as the beautiful golden haired goddess nodded to her before carefully raising her hand, lifting Tia up into the air. Tia stood up, holding onto one of the long, slender fingers for balance and looked around her. Slowly, her people began to kneel down in reverence of the creature and Tia's courage to communicate with it. Only when her brother knelt as well did Tia turn to face the goddess who came from above with a smile on her tiny face.

Jett slipped out of the dark passage and climbed down until he could see what was going on more clearly. The passage opened out near the smallest waterfall and onto the ledge that ran along the edge of it. It would be a quick climb down to the balcony of the palace where he often saw the slender green female standing and looking out over her kingdom.

His eyes suddenly widened in concern when he saw the huge golden giant sitting in the middle of the red moss field. A low growl escaped him and his hand tightened on the short sword he carried at his waist when he saw the creature lifting his bride. His lips drew back to show his small sharp teeth as he fought the urge to attack it. He would if it harmed the female he knew belonged to him. He didn't care how big it was, he would destroy it.

Moving along the side of the cliff, he nimbly began the climb down until he was a few feet above the balcony of the palace. He pushed off, landing silently on the spacious ledge. He turned as he landed, his knees bent and one hand stretched out to balance him before he stood.

Moving into the shadows, he watched as the events below unfolded. He had to hide behind the thick curtains when three of the armed soldiers returned briefly to the palace only to return to his bride and the creature holding her in the palm of its huge hand.

Jett watched as his bride presented the creature with a glowing, red stone. He sucked in a breath when he realized he could understand what the creature was saying after she placed it around her neck.

"My name is Ariel," the creature replied with a soft chuckle.

"I am called Tia." Jett's breath left him in a hiss of painful desire when he heard Tia's name for the first time. He leaned forward, trying to get a better view. "I am the Keeper of the Stories. This is my brother, Tamblin. He is our leader," Tia replied in a silky voice that sent waves of heat rushing through him.

Jett smiled, Tia – a beautiful name for a beautiful woman. He continued to watch from his viewpoint, gaining confidence that the creature meant no harm to his bride or her people as he listened to her talk. He debated whether to follow when the creature stood and Tia, Tamblin, and many of his soldiers moved away but decided against it. They would return, of that he was confident.

No, now would be a good time to explore my bride's home and pack a few things that she might need, he decided.

Jett moved silently through the empty palace, exploring one level after another until he came to a room he knew must belong to Tia. He let the long curtain doorway fall behind him as he gently touched the delicate fabrics hanging on the walls. He breathed in, inhaling her fragrant scent. It made him think of the wild flowers that bloomed briefly after the heavy rains. He ran his tawny fingers over the silky woven lengths of cloth that she wrapped around her body. He couldn't help but imagine what it was going to be like when he unwove it from her slender frame.

Scooping up several long lengths, he quickly bundled them up so that they would be easy to carry. Inside of the bundle, he rolled the comb she used on her bright red hair and several delicate hair combs. He would have to make her more.

Combs made from the sands were beautiful and would look good against her silky strands. He pulled back the last tapestry hanging on the wall and discovered shelves filled with carefully rolled scrolls. Pulling out the one on top, he walked over to the low table in the center of the room and unrolled it. Inscribed on the thick fiber paper were images depicting different scenes. Each was done with delicate strokes filled with the same vibrant colors that reminded Jett of his beloved.

His eyes moved to the writing below them. He frowned as he concentrated. It was difficult, but he was slowly able to decipher the words. They were in the ancient language his mother and father taught him when he was young.

"What are you doing?" Tia's outraged voice sounded from the doorway. "Who are you? How did you get into my rooms?"

Jett had been so absorbed in deciphering the scroll and the tale it was telling that he had let his guard down. Now, instead of him having the element of surprise, his bride did. He took a quick step back from the table. He couldn't help but grin as his bride, upset that he had been reading her scroll, made the mistake of marching over to the table instead of calling for help or running away.

The moment she was within reach, he wrapped his arms around her trembling body. "Do not fear, my heart. I have not come to harm you, but to claim you," he breathed out in her ear.

Tia jerked in surprise, her eyes widening as she stared up at him, startled. "What do you mean - claim me?" she asked, bewildered.

Jett chuckled at her innocent look of confusion. He couldn't resist leaning down and brushing his lips briefly against hers. Her startled gasp pulled a groan from him and he took her lips in a savage kiss that spoke of his desire. He had wanted to do this since he first saw her several months ago.

Tia pushed weakly against his broad chest until he reluctantly lifted his head. "What do you think you are doing?" she gasped breathlessly, looking up at him with huge, confused eyes.

Jett smiled mischievously. "I thought that was a bit obvious! I'm claiming you as my bride."

CHAPTER THREE

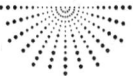

ia didn't know how to respond to the larger male who had invaded her personal domain. She had never seen anyone like him before. He was tall, even taller than her brother. He was also not the same soft shade of green that most of her clan was.

He was a dark, tawny color with rich dark brown hair that fell in long, braided ropes down his back almost to his waist. His eyes were a light violet, almost identical to the water that flowed from the rocky walls of their home. He did not wear clothing like them, either. A blush heightened the color of her cheeks as her hands slid over the bare flesh of his shoulders. The only thing covering him was a pair of light brown pants tucked into a darker brown pair of ankle boots.

"I am not your bride," Tia snapped out, upset that she let this strange man shake her normal calm. "You will leave immediately or I will summon my brother and the guards!"

Jett grinned down at her, letting his hands span her tiny waist. "Of course, my lady, I will be happy to leave immediately," he said with a playful kiss to her lips.

He chuckled at Tia's outraged gasp when he lifted her gently up and balanced her on his shoulder so he could grab the things he had packed for her in his other hand. Keeping his arm around her thighs, he listened carefully before drawing the curtain leading out to the balcony aside. He jumped up onto the ledge, balancing before he murmured for her to hang on and not fight him.

"What are you doing?" Tia gasped again as she stared fearfully down at the long drop to the ground below them. She tried to cling to him, but didn't have any way to really hold on so she remained frozen. "You are going to kill us!" she whispered hoarsely.

Jett laughed as he nimbly began climbing up the side of the cliff to the ledge where the crack to the tunnel was. "You haven't been talking with Santil, have you? He said the same thing!"

Tia frowned, thinking hard before she shook her head. "I don't know a Santil. Where does he live?" she asked, unable to contain her curiosity.

"In the Kingdom of the Sand People," Jett replied, pulling himself up far enough to set her down on the ledge before he pulled himself up onto it. "That is where I am taking you."

Tia looked at the huge tawny figure standing over her with her mouth opened. He really meant it when he said he was claiming her. Her heart did a little quiver and began to beat faster, but for once she wondered if it was because of her sickness or because of his words.

She looked out over the cavern filled with the richness of the mushroom forests and the glittering stones that gave them life. The thought of leaving her safe world should have terrified her but it didn't. Her eyes moved to look up at the powerful figure standing over hers and inside she felt a wave of longing.

She knew she didn't have long to live. She had resigned herself to live her remaining time quietly reviewing the stories she had illustrated and retold. The fact that she would not live long enough to have children of her own caused a sharp pain to flair through her.

Her death would mean the end of the line of the Keeper of the Stories. That was why she felt it was so important to pass on her knowledge the only way she could. Her eyes traveled down to the balcony to her rooms.

She had finished all the stories that she knew. There really was nothing left for her here. Perhaps, this was the gods and goddesses way of letting her see what was beyond her home before her heart no longer beat.

Jett stepped closer to where she was sitting and knelt on one knee before her. He brushed a strand of her wayward hair back tenderly before cupping her chin. He waited until her eyes once more looked deeply into his.

"Come with me," he whispered, holding out his hand. "Let me show you my world."

Tia bit her lip and studied him for a moment before she let her eyes sweep over the cavern one last time. "I didn't get to say goodbye to Tamblin," she answered reluctantly.

"It is not goodbye," Jett promised her. "I will bring you back whenever you wish to visit."

Tia knew deep down there would be no coming back once she left. She knew Tamblin would be upset when he discovered her missing. She could only hope that he would understand when he saw the scrolls and read through them. When he did, he would discover the note she had left for him among them. She had not planned on him finding it before her death, but what did it matter whether she was dead or not. In the end, it would not change her outcome.

Tia turned back to look at the unusual, but handsome male kneeling in front of her and laid her trembling hand in his strong, firm one. "I will come with you," she breathed out with a small excited smile.

Jett leaned in, brushing his lips across hers before pulling her up with a joyful laugh. "You will not regret it, I swear. I will show you the most wondrous sights!" he exclaimed joyfully as he wrapped his hands around her tiny waist and lifted her up, swinging her around with a shout of joy.

Tia laughed breathlessly as he set her back onto her feet. He gripped her hand firmly but gently in his and pulled her toward the narrow opening. Tia glanced back briefly over her shoulder as he pulled her through before focusing on the new path she was taking.

CHAPTER FOUR

*S*antil shook his head when he saw Jett emerge out of the darkness with a slender green female. "You are going to start a war, you know," Santil said with a sigh.

Jett laughed, looking down in amusement at Tia. "Meet Santil. He is always thinking the worse is going to happen."

"That is because it usually does," Santil snorted, scowling. "Jett is forever getting us in trouble."

"Jett," Tia said softly with a smile. "I like that name," she said shyly, staring up at the huge male that took her breath away.

Santil stopped at the opening of the tunnel and looked at his large friend in disbelief. "You kidnapped her and didn't even bother to tell her your name? That is low, even for you, my friend," he joked before turning back to make sure the coast was clear of any predators.

"Ignore him," Jett teased back, jumping down behind his friend and opening his arms for her. "I try to." Tia couldn't help but giggle at the way the two unusual men picked on each other.

It was so different from Tamblin and the elders. Only the children seemed to have a sense of humor anymore, she thought sadly.

Tia shielded her eyes from the brightness that she had only heard about. She had never seen the top side of their world. Tamblin had refused her many requests, saying it was too dangerous. She blinked rapidly until her eyes adjusted enough so that she could see without her eyes tearing.

It was big and beautiful. As far as she could see there were rolling waves of glittering, windswept sand. She tried to imagine what it would have looked like before when the large mushroom forests covered it but couldn't.

"Come," Jett said with a soft smile of encouragement. "We need to make haste if we are to return to our home before the darkness falls."

Santil shuddered. "I agree. I don't want to have to deal with the night creatures on top of everything else."

"What else is there?" Tia asked curiously as she put her hands on Jett's broad shoulder to steady herself as he lowered her down to the ground.

A warm shiver swept down her spine and she couldn't resist looking up at him to see if he felt her reaction. The heated look in his eyes showed he was not immune to her touch either. A rosy blush rose up her cheeks as unfamiliar feelings coursed through her.

"Sand worms," Jett and Santil said at the same time, answering the question she had already forgotten she had asked.

"But, you needn't worry," Jett said, guiding her to a small machine with a long seat and odd shaped wings. He helped her on before sliding behind her so he could keep one arm wrapped protectively around her. "I'll keep you safe," he murmured in her ear enjoying how the tiny points twitched and a light dusky rose color flushed her cheeks.

～

Tia loved the journey to the Kingdom of the Sand. It had taken them until dusk to reach it. Her first view had been of the huge clear, glittering dome set upon a high rocky surface. As they skimmed across the sands, more details began to emerge. She could see the shape of a huge castle built into the center of the rock face. It was surrounded by large turrets on each corner.

Tia pressed a hand to her chest as her heart stuttered and stopped. She tried to draw in a deep breath, but couldn't. The hand gripping Jett's arm tightened in panic as she feared her time had come to an end just when she was getting a chance to experience her first true adventure. Jett's arm squeezed her and she felt his warm breath against her neck just as her heart restarted sluggishly at first before picking up its uneven rhythm again.

"Welcome to Sandora," Jett whispered in her ear.

Tia nodded, unable to speak for the lump in her throat. Instead, she squeezed his arm to let him know she heard him. The light skimmers sped down a long tunnel that opened up at their approach. Tia looked over her shoulder trying to see but couldn't because of Jett's larger frame.

"The tunnel collapses behind us so nothing else can come in behind us," he explained with an understanding smile. "Hang on," he said.

He tightened his hold on her before pushing down his feet on the accelerator, sending the skimmer speeding through the tunnel until it burst through high above the walls of the city below them. He shouted with joy as he flew in and out of the narrow tubes that formed walkways between buildings. He didn't slow down until he reached the outer corridor leading into the palace.

They swept through a long, dark tunnel before coming out into a wide area filled with men, women, and skimmers. Santil floated down beside them a moment later with a huge grin on his face. Jett jumped off the skimmer, sweeping Tia up into his arms.

Tia squealed in alarm before wrapping her arms tightly around his neck. "I can walk," she said breathlessly even as she snuggled closer to his warm body.

Jett smiled tenderly down at her and shook his head, sending his long braids dancing around him in waves. "I know but I like carrying you," he teased. "I don't ever want to put you down."

Tia rolled her big brown eyes at him. "You would just tire yourself out," she snorted but couldn't quite hide her amused smile.

"I'd like to see that!" Santil said, coming up beside them and slapping Jett on the back of his head before dancing away out of Jett's reach. "His mother, father, sister, and brothers have been trying to do that since the day he was born!"

"Like you are any better!" Jett retorted with a playful snap of his teeth.

"Jett!" a loud, deep voice called out harshly.

Santil grimaced before raising his hand and saluting Jett and Tia. "That is my signal to disappear. It has been a pleasure to meet the one who could capture this mongrel's attention, my lady," he said before disappearing between two outer buildings.

Tia watched wide-eyed as a figure as imposing as Jett's walked down a set of steps towards them. The man was dressed in a pair of dark brown pants with a black vest that left much of his chest exposed. Around his waist he carried two swords that swayed as he strode toward them. His hair was as long as Jett's and braided in long dark brown ropes that flowed gracefully behind him as he walked.

"Who is that?" she asked in a hushed whisper, watching the huge male approach with a fierce scowl upon his face.

"My father," Jett grinned. "He only looks scary, but he really isn't."

Tia ducked her head to hide her giggle before she raised it to look at the man as he came to a stop in front of them. "Who is this?" Roan asked, looking at Tia with a puzzled expression on his face. "Why is she green?"

Tia looked at the man with a stubborn tilt to her chin. "Why aren't you?" she asked back with a raised eyebrow.

Roan stared at the female for a moment before he burst out laughing. "I have no idea. I will have to ask my mother," he responded in amusement. "Roan, King of the Sand Kingdom at your service," he added with a graceful bow.

Tia giggled. "I am called Tia. Keeper of the Stories for the Kingdom of Glitter," she responded with a shy smile. "It is indeed a pleasure to meet you, your Grace."

"Jett?" Roan asked, staring into Tia's unusual but beautiful face.

"I've claimed her," Jett responded to the unspoken question. "She is my bride."

Roan started in surprise before a large grin lit his face up. "At last," he murmured before he turned and bellowed out in a voice that ricocheted around the high walls of the palace. "Jett has taken a bride!" he proclaimed to all standing within hearing distance.

Loud cheers followed his announcement, stunning Tia who stared in awe as men and women gathered around them cheering. "What is going on?" she whispered, trying to sink down into Jett's arms. "What did he mean, you have taken a bride? I heard you say that before, but I am not familiar with the word," she said, looking nervously up at him.

Jett leaned over and whispered in her ear so she could hear him above the roar of the crowds. Tia paled as the meaning sank in. She looked up at him, tears filling her eyes as the realization of what was happening overwhelmed her.

She had to tell him it was impossible. There was no way she could be his bride as much as she wished she could be. She did not understand how it worked for his people, but for hers the loss of a mate could have devastating consequences.

Her heart beat frantically, stuttering and stopping before repeating the erratic rhythm over and over until she was trembling and had turned a deathly pale green. Her eyes drooped at the effort to keep them open.

Her breath came in tiny gasps as her weak heart worked frantically in her chest.

"My lords! Strangers approach!" one of the guards yelled down.

Tia felt her vision blurring and tried to calm the panic. Her heart slowed, but continued to skip, leaving her weak. She turned to stare up at the top of the clear dome, recognizing the flying beast from home and the colors of her brother's armor. Turning her head, she let it fall weakly back against Jett's broad chest, seeking comfort from his strength.

Roan turned to look up at the clear dome as well. Even in the dim light, he could see the flying creatures with warriors guiding them as they hovered around the top of the Kingdom. He ordered his men to their skimmers and to prepare for battle.

"Wait!" Jett's voice rose over the mayhem. "What did you say, Tia?" he asked, concerned by her sudden pale complexion.

"It is Tamblin," she said weakly. "I must... see him... one... last... time," she murmured in a voice barely loud enough to be heard.

"Tia, what is it, my love? What do you mean one last time? What is wrong?" Jett asked fearfully, pulling her closer to his chest as he gazed down at her pale complexion.

Tia forced her eyes open so she could look into Jett's handsome features. "I'm dying," she forced out. "I..." Tears filled her eyes and overflowed down her pale cheeks. "I.... cannot be.... your bride."

"No," Jett cried out hoarsely, looking to his father who heard the quiet words. "No, she cannot die. I love her," he croaked out to his father in fear.

Roan looked at his son's ashen face before gazing at the slender figure cradled protectively against his youngest son's body. "There is a way to save her. Take her to the healing chamber," he said, his face set in determination. He turned to his head guard. "Open the tunnel," he ordered as he climbed onto his skimmer.

Jett watched his father rise up to fly over the walls of the palace. He pulled Tia closer to his body and strode for the entrance. He looked up at the door as he climbed the steps. His mother stood looking down at him with tears of compassion glimmering in her eyes. He felt her hand brush over his arm gently as he passed her.

"She will live if that is your decision," his mother said quietly.

"It is," Jett said, striding down the long corridor toward the entrance to the healing chambers buried deep under the palace.

Tia drifted in and out of consciousness as her tiny heart struggled. Jett's tender touch soothed her fears and a sense of peace settled over her. She would not be alone when she died. That had been one of her greatest fears. She heard voices in the background. At times they rose in anger before a gentle voice spoke.

"You understand what this means," Roan said heavily as he looked at his son.

"Jett?" His mother reached out and touched his arm in fear and worry.

Jett turned his head to look at his mother and shook his head. "You do not understand. I knew the moment I saw her, she was for me."

Tamblin stepped forward; helpless rage twisted his features as he stared at the pale face of his beloved sister. "What do you mean she was for you? You did not even know her until today!" he bit out angrily. "Why did you take her? The excitement of being taken from her home is too much for her. Return her to me and let me take her home. At least she will die among her people!"

"No," Jett said, rising angrily and pulling his sword. "She is mine and will remain by my side!"

"What can you do?" Tamblin yelled as he took a step closer to Jett.

"What can you do that we haven't? There is nothing we can do to save her," he said, anger and grief choking him as he stared at the tall male who stood protectively over Tia.

Jett's jaw clenched and he looked at the glowing waters of their healing pool. As with all things in life, there had to be a balance with death. There could not be one without the other. The healing pools demanded such balance. The healing waters would not work if the balance was not maintained. Jett could not ask another to give their life in exchange for Tia. The only way the pools could save one as sick as her was if another life was sacrificed so that its power was replenished, keeping the balance between life and death.

Jett looked at Tamblin before turning to gaze tenderly down at Tia's still form. "I would give anything to save her," he responded quietly before letting his sword drop to the floor of the chamber. "I would give anything… including my life."

Tamblin fell backwards in confusion at the sudden change in the male in front of him. Jett didn't give Tia's brother a chance to protest. He gently scooped Tia up into his arms, smiling down at her still, pale face. He bent his head closer to her and brushed a soft kiss over her lips.

"I love you, Tia," he murmured quietly, forgetting everyone else in the large chamber. "I give to you my heart, so that it may beat strongly for you. I give to you my strength so you never feel weak, and I give to you my love, so you will know the joy you have given me by just existing."

Jett walked down the steps and into the swirling blue and silver waters of the pool, moving slowly until it covered Tia up to her chin. Taking a deep breath, he pressed his lips against hers one last time and slowly sank down under the shimmering surface.

CHAPTER FIVE

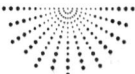

$\mathcal{T}$ia felt waves of warmth flowing through her body. At first, she thought it was strange as she had been so cold before. Her heartbeat grew stronger as the warmth encircled her. She could feel Jett surrounding her with his love as well as his arms.

Shimmering lights danced behind her eyelids as images of them together formed. It was as if she could see their life together. His eyes turning with laughter to her as he held one of their children in his strong arms as another clung to his leg.

She could feel his strong arms holding her in the darkness as he listened to her tell him of her visions. She could feel the joy of him taking her on his skimmer through the lush mushroom forests that would soon cover their world again. In those few precious moments, she saw what she thought she would never have.

Tia felt strength suffusing her. It filled her body and a sense of peace and happiness at being whole again swept through her. She fought the urge to cry out when the lips pressed against hers suddenly fell away, waking her from the web of dreams she had been caught in. She opened her eyes under the swirling water, her feelings of joy turning to fear and despair when she saw Jett's still, peaceful face floating before her.

Her hands went frantically to his face, cupping his cheeks and holding him. Fear unlike anything she had ever known made her press her lips to his in a desperate attempt to wake him even as her hands moved to his chest. Under her palms, his heart stuttered and stilled.

NO! she screamed silently. *I won't let you do this. I love you. You claimed me,* she sobbed silently. *How can I be your bride if you are not with me? How can my dreams become reality without you by my side? How can you hold our children if you are not there to give them to me? Please, no. Please, please, please, don't leave me alone,* she begged, pressing her lips frantically to his again in an effort to give him back what he had given to her. *I don't want your gift without you. You promised me strength, but I am weak without your arms around me. You promised me joy, but there is nothing but sadness without you there to make me laugh. You promised me your heart, but without you it is empty. Please come back to me. I love you. Only together can I be strong. Only together can I find joy. Only together can we find love.*

Tia closed her eyes, wrapping her arms and legs around Jett's still, life-less body. She gave herself to the swirling waters. She had no desire to live a half-life. If the gods and goddesses would take his life in exchange for hers then she would give them both of their souls so they could be as one for eternity.

Twisting her fingers through his long, braided ropes of hair, she let their bodies sink further under the dark blue and silver liquid. A sense of peace and acceptance settled over her. She would not die alone and she would not leave him.

"Keeper of the Stories," a soothing voice echoed through her mind and resonated through her soul. *"Do you not remember the story of the great warrior?"*

Tia stirred as the vivid images flooded her mind. Imagines of a great warrior who was said to have fallen in love with a gentle girl from another tribe. Her mother's voice flowed over her as the pictures danced through her mind.

"Remember, Tia," her mother scolded her when she drifted off instead of paying attention. "Only when the warrior gives the ultimate sacrifice will the gods and goddesses gift them with their hearts' desire."

"What is that, momma?" a tiny Tia asked, turning her large brown eyes in curiosity to her mother.

"He will give his heart to save her and she will refuse to accept it unless he keeps it safe for her," her mother replied, stroking her hair.

"Does that make her a warrior too?" the childlike Tia asked. "If she fights for him, will that make her a warrior?"

"Of course, little one," her mother said soothingly. "How can there be love if only one heart beats?"

Tia felt her body drifting upward, carried by the strong arms that surrounded her. *I remember, momma,* she thought. *I remember.*

Tia's eyes fluttered open as the healing waters fell away from her. She stared up into the light violet eyes of Jett, who smiled tenderly down at her as he carried her out of the healing pool. She reached a trembling hand up to lightly trace his cheek with her fingertips. An answering smile curved her lips.

"You are my warrior," she murmured in awe, her eyes shining with love. "You are the warrior who would give his heart to me."

Jett gazed down into her softly glowing eyes. "I would do anything for your love, Tia," he said huskily. "You are my life."

"As you are mine," Tia replied, knowing that the vision she had of their life together would soon become a reality.

Author's Note:

I hope you enjoyed the story of Tia and Jett. These characters were first introduced in Ambushing Ariel: Dragon Lords of Valdier Book 4. I never expected to write them into Ariel's story, but once I did, I became fascinated with their characters. I feel all characters deserve to have their stories told if they wish to share it with me. Perhaps Tamblin might wish to share his story as well. I hope so.

~ S. E. Smith

See your favorite characters again in:
The Dragonlings and the Magic Four-Leaf Clover

A little magic can go a long way....

A campfire tale has the dragonlings and their besties enchanted with a mythical kingdom called Glitter, home of the magical, mischievous Great King Leprechaun and the Little People. When their dads disappear, they are certain King Leprechaun is responsible. Armed with a magic four-leaf clover, the younglings will do anything to save their fathers, including tricking the King by using their golden symbiots—because everyone knows a Leprechaun can't resist gold!

THE DRAGONLINGS AND THE MAGIC FOUR-LEAF CLOVER

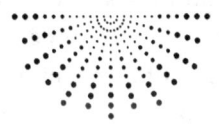

CAST OF CHARACTERS

For those who have not yet read the Dragon Lords of Valdier series, here is a little background.

The Valdier are dragon shifters. Only the Valdier and their mates can bond with the mysterious and powerful golden symbiots, who are, yes, symbiotic creatures, and they are stand-out characters all on their own! Each Valdier consists of three parts: the dragon, the man/woman, and their symbiot companion. They are friends with the Curizan (a species able to harness the energy around them) and the Sarafin (a cat shifting species). The following is a character guide for those new to the series:

Zoran Reykill, Leader of the Valdier **true mate to** Abby Tanner:
one son: Zohar
Zoran's symbiot: Goldie
Zohar's symbiot: Truck

Mandra Reykill **true mate to** Ariel Hamm:
one son: Jabir
Mandra's symbiot: Precious
Jabir's symbiot: Munch

Kelan Reykill **true mate to** Trisha Grove:
one son: Bálint
Kelan's symbiot: Bio
Bálint's symbiot: Tag

Trelon Reykill **true mate to** Cara Truman:
twin daughters: Amber and Jade
one son: James
Trelon's symbiot: Symba
Amber's symbiot: Treat

Jade's symbiot: Trix

Creon Reykill **true mate to** Carmen Walker:
twin daughters: Spring and Phoenix
Creon's symbiot: Harvey
Phoenix's symbiot: Stardust
Spring's symbiot: Little Bit

Paul Grove **true mate to** Morian Reykill:
one daughter: Morah
Paul and Morian's symbiot: Crash
Morah's symbiot: Princess Buttercup

Cree and Calo Aryeh **true mates to** Melina Franklin:
one daughter: Hope
Calo's symbiot: Teddy
Cree's symbiot: Bear
Hope's symbiot: Rainbow

Vox d'Rojah, King of the Sarafin **mated to** Riley St. Claire:
one son: Roam
twin daughters: Sacha and Pearl

Viper d'Rojah **mated to** Tina St. Claire:
one son: Leo

Asim Kemark **true mate to** Pearl St. Claire

Ha'ven Ha'darra, Prince of the Curizan **mated to** Emma Watson:
one daughter: Alice

Aikaterina: Unknown species; accepted as a Goddess to the Valdier,
she is the oldest and most powerful of her kind.

Arilla and Arosa: Unknown species, still young for their kind, they are
twins and thought to be Goddesses.

CHAPTER ONE

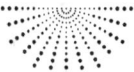

*M*orian stood in the dining room of their Valdier palace residence watching her mate, Paul Grove, carefully inventory and pack the assembled items he needed into a large backpack. In the background, she could hear their daughter, Morah, animatedly talking to her symbiot, Princess Buttercup. The excitement in Morah's voice was impossible to ignore, as were Morian's misgivings about Paul and Morah's upcoming camping trip.

"Paul, are you sure about this?" she asked in a voice filled with doubt.

Paul looked over at her with a startled expression. Laying a rope down on the table, he straightened, held his arms open wide, and gave her that self-assured smile that always melted her heart. Walking toward him, she slipped her arms around his waist and pressed a kiss to his lips.

He looked down at her. "You know that I'll take good care of Morah. I won't let anything happen to her," he promised.

Morian raised a delicate eyebrow. "What makes you think I'm talking about her? I'm not in the least bit worried about Morah and the other children, or even about you. I know you'll be fine," she replied with a soft chuckle.

Paul frowned. "Then what are you worried about?" he asked, puzzled.

"The other men! You, Morah, and the other younglings will be out in the woods with *all* of my sons as well as Vox and Ha'ven. *That* is what I am worried about," she grumbled, pressing a kiss to the tip of his nose.

She felt the chuckle that shook his muscular frame. "Don't forget Cree, Calo, and Viper. Zoran warned me that they are coming as well. I've dealt with a lot of young men out in the woods during my time. I think I can handle your sons and the other men," he reassured her.

Both of them looked around when they heard the loud sounds of items hitting the floor. The clanging and banging reminded him of a heavy rain on a tin roof. It was followed by childish mutterings and the sound of something dragging along the floor.

"Dada, I's ready to goes camping," Morah breathlessly called to him from the living room.

Morian looked at Paul with a wary expression when they heard another loud crash. She stepped out of his arms and hurried into the living room. She stopped when she saw Morah standing with her tiny hands on her dainty little hips. Morah's small symbiot had dropped the bag it was trying to carry and spilled toys all over the floor. A choked laugh caught in her throat, and she had to raise her hand to cover her mouth and stifle her laughter.

"I tolds you that you's was going to spill it if you pulls it that way," Morah said with a shake of her head.

The symbiot picked up a bright red ball in its mouth and grinned around it. Morah tugged on the ball. She inelegantly fell to the floor in a small heap of pink and red silk and lace. Her black curls bounced from under her pointed hat. Rolling to her feet, her cheeks rosy and her dark golden eyes sparkling, she stuck her tongue out at her symbiot before impatiently waving her hand at the mess.

"You gots to help pick them up," she ordered, looking sternly at

Princess Buttercup before she bent over and started picking up the toys.

Morian chuckled and turned her head to glance at Paul when he came up behind her to peer over her shoulder at their daughter. His muffled laugh tickled her ear. Morah was ready, alright. She looked as if she had packed just about every single one of her toys in every bag she could find in her room, which included a small bag that Paul had made for her and one of her pillow cases as well.

"I think she plans to take all of her toys," Morian murmured.

"I think she packed up her entire room," Paul groaned with a rueful shake of his head when he saw several 'Princess' dresses in various colors spilling out of one bag.

Morian bit her lip when Morah adjusted the bright pink princess hat on her head to keep it from slipping off. Ever since Cara had told the girls the stories about the princesses from their human world, Morah had been in love with them. Her current thing was dressing up with the tall, medieval style hats and the matching long frilly dresses that resembled the gowns once worn on Earth. Even her dolls were dressed up like miniature princesses.

Paul shook his head. "Trisha was such a tomboy. I couldn't get her in a dress. It is going to be World War III getting Morah out of one," he groaned.

Morian lifted her hand and ran it down Paul's cheek. "I'll get her ready while you repack the things she can actually take. Just remember to pack a couple of her dolls or you'll be coming back early," she warned with a wink.

"Dolls... Which ones?" Paul muttered, gazing at the long trail of toys that littered the hallway from Morah's bedroom all the way to the living room.

Morian laughed. "Pick anything in pink or red and hope she doesn't decide green and blue are her new favorite colors in the meantime," she teased before turning her attention to Morah. "How about I help you and Princess Buttercup get ready to go camping?"

Morian didn't wait for a response. She scooped the tiny girl up into her arms and headed back to Morah's bedroom. Holding her close, Morian buried her face against Morah's neck and blew raspberries against it. Morah melted into a fit of giggles.

"I's going camping with Dada!" Morah announced with gleeful excitement.

"I know you are. You are going with your uncles and cousins, too," Morian reminded her daughter.

"Is Hope and Leo coming's too?" Morah asked with an anxious plea.

"Yes, they are going camping, too," she promised, brushing the dark curls back from Morah's face.

"Are's we going on another ad... addie... addieventure?" Morah asked.

This time Morah's eyes were filled with excited hope. Morian bit back her laughter. It was a good thing Paul wasn't in the bedroom with them, or he might change his mind about this sudden crazy adventure. This camping expedition had grown from a father-daughter overnight camping trip to a three-day event complete with all the younglings and their fathers.

She and the other women had given up on talking the Reykill brothers and their friends out of going because every time they attempted to dissuade their stubborn mates, it seemed one of the warriors would invite someone else to join the expedition. Now, even the twin dragons and Vox's brother, Viper, were going camping.

"Listen," Riley had commented earlier when they found out about the latest additions to the group of campers. "If the kids could go on an adventure down rivers and up mountains on their own, I'm sure they can handle three days in the woods with their dads."

Morian didn't point out that during that adventure, a mountain blew up or that if it hadn't been for Christoff, the Old Dragon of the Mountain, the children and even some of the adults might not have survived that particular adventure. The only positive thing was that none of the women were going. That meant there was less chance that a holiday tale would send the kids off on another misadventure.

Morah was still talking about the Great Easter Bunny adventure that she had been a part of and how they had stopped the giant bunnies from taking Jabir's big eggs. She needed to keep reminding herself that they would only be gone for three days—and that Paul would be with them.

"Mommy," Morah asked, cupping Morian's face.

She looked down at her daughter and smiled. "Yes, my little princess?" Morian replied.

"Will you be alrights while Dada and I is gone?" Morah asked with a worried frown.

Morian smiled and bent to press a kiss to Morah's cheek. "I'll be just fine. It is your Dada that I'm worried about," she chuckled.

Morah lifted her chin. "I's going to take cares of Dada. I won't lets nothing happens to him. I promise as a princess," she declared with a toss of her head.

Morian reached out and caught the pointed hat as it fell off of Morah's head. She tickled Morah's ribs, laughing when the little girl squealed in delight. Once again, she reassured herself that everything would be alright—after all, there couldn't possibly be any Earth holidays at this time of year!

CHAPTER TWO

*R*iley watched the group of men in the courtyard with misgivings. Vox was packing the camping gear into a smaller pack while growling under his breath. She bit her lip and hugged little Pearl against her.

"You'd think the guys would know better," Tina said, placing Riley's other daughter, Sacha, on the ground.

Riley sighed and set little Pearl down next to her sister. Of course, the cubs immediately shifted into their leopards and headed for their father. If she wasn't careful, the twins would find a way to sneak into their dad's backpack.

"What do you mean—the fact that all the guys are going camping, or the fact that they are taking the kids?" Riley asked in a distracted voice.

"That my dad would allow them to take all of their luxury items," Trisha laughed. "I swear they are as bad as the kids when it comes to packing."

Riley rolled her eyes. "Vox kept making excuses that this, that, and the other was for Roam. Roam couldn't care less. He'd be happy if Spring just dug a hole in the ground, so they could climb into it. I guess she did that once before," she commented.

"Or up a tree. Speaking of which, I need to go get my son out of one," Tina added, watching the small, black tiger cub trying to grasp the bark of a nearby tree. "Leo, you'd better not! Viper!"

The tiger cub turned to look at his mother before scurrying up the trunk to the first branch. Riley watched her sister take off after her son. She breathed a sigh of relief at the fact that Sacha and Pearl weren't as adventurous as their big brother, or their cousin. Looking down, she frowned when she saw that her twin daughters were gone.

"Dammit! Those two better not get as bad as Cara's girls when it comes to getting into mischief," Riley said, frantically looking for the twins.

"They're okay, Riley. They are playing with Morah and Hope," Abby said, nodding toward the group of little girls where they were sitting in the grass playing with several dolls.

"Thank goodness. Those two are definitely daddy's girls. They love being with Vox. If I'm not careful, they'll climb into a bag and bury themselves. The next three days are going to be a challenge to keep them entertained," Riley said before her face lit up with excitement. "I think I'll take them to see Great-Grandma and Asim. They love going up to their house."

"I'm sure the emus would love that," Ariel quipped in a dry tone.

"Well, I think we should all go up to Ariel and Mandra's house. Wouldn't that be a lovely get-away?" Abby suggested, looping her arm through Ariel's.

Carmen laughed. "You're just saying that because you know the guys are going to be camping in the forest near there, and you are worried about the kids," she said with a knowing smile.

Abby shrugged one elegant shoulder. "I guess you're right. After all, what could possibly happen?" she asked with an amused grin as she waved a hand toward the boys who were huddled together.

A grimace crossed Carmen's face when she saw Spring's head pop up in the middle of the group, followed by Amber and Jade. The little girl glanced around before she waved to Phoenix to join her. It was obvious to all of the mothers that the kids were already up to something and plotting like crazy.

"I agree with Abby, I think we should all go hang out at Ariel and Mandra's mountain home," Carmen said with a sheepish grin.

"All in favor, say 'aye'," Abby said, looking along the line of women.

"Aye," they all agreed.

"I'll say a double 'Aye' for Tina since she is busy," Riley replied before she frowned. "Okay, where did those two girls of mine disappear to this time? Pearl! Sacha! Yum-yum time!"

Everyone turned when they heard a loud purr coming from the men's direction. Glancing around, they looked puzzled until they saw Riley's red face and Vox striding toward her with a very predatory grin on his face. Riley backed up, held out her hand, and shook her head.

"Vox, don't you....! You mangy cat! It is.... Tina... Please watch the girls!" Riley squeaked when Vox lifted her up in his arms and kept walking toward the palace.

Cara, who had been coming down the path with one of her new inventions, quickly stepped to the side and watched as Vox strode by with Riley in his arms. She walked toward the group with a puzzled frown.

"What was all that about?" Cara asked.

Morian's lips twitched. "I believe Riley is still nursing the twins," she answered, watching the twins playing with Morah and Hope again now that their dad had left.

"Nursing?" Cara repeated before her eyes widened, and she burst out laughing. "Oh! Well, they say cats love fresh milk."

"So do dragons," Morian warned with a twinkle of amusement at Cara.

"Tell me about it," Cara retorted, turning to watch Trelon with a soft expression.

CHAPTER THREE

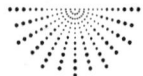

*L*ater that afternoon, Paul watched the men as they worked together to set up camp. He had laughed when he and the symbiots were assigned the task of watching over the children. He could already see the expressions of doubt creeping into the men's eyes about the wisdom of taking this many children out camping on their own. Looking down, he swept his gaze over the sea of eyes watching him with expectation and barely contained excitement.

"Okay, first things first. We need firewood. Now, the key to finding good firewood is picking different sizes and making sure the wood is neither too wet nor too old and rotted," he explained.

A hand immediately went up. "Yes, Leo," Paul acknowledged.

"Can I eats it?" the little boy with dark-brown eyes, like his mother, asked.

Paul shot a warning glance to the older dragonlings when they started to laugh. They quickly grew quiet. He shook his head.

"No, I wouldn't recommend eating the wood," he said.

Morah turned to look at Leo. "They mights have bugs in it," she said.

"But... I likes to eat bugs," Leo responded with a disappointed expression.

"I like to eat them, too, Leo," Roam loudly whispered to his cousin.

"Ew!" Hope said, wiggling her nose in distaste.

"You won't have to eat bugs, Hope. I'll share my food with you," Jabir offered, a shy smile on his face. "I don't have any bugs or meat in the food my mom packed."

"Hope, do you want to help us?" Cree called.

"No's, I's having funs," she replied with an infectious smile.

Paul looked up to see Cree scowling over at the small group. The reason for Cree's displeasure took a moment to sink in. It wasn't until he followed the other man's gaze that he saw Jabir smiling at Hope. Fortunately, the little girl appeared to be oblivious to her dad's consternation.

This is going to be a long three days, he thought with a silent chuckle.

"Okay, who wants to help me get the firewood?" he asked, rubbing his hands together in expectation.

Seconds later, he was shaking his head. All of the little ones were scattering like flies at a Fourth of July picnic. Only Morah remained—for a brief moment. She gave him an apologetic smile before she shifted into her dragon and bounded off after the other kids.

"I'll help you gather some wood," Mandra said. "Cree has decided he wants to keep an eye on Hope and my boy," he chuckled.

"You don't look too concerned," Paul observed.

Mandra shook his head. "I know how futile it would be to try to keep them apart if they are destined to be true mates. I'd rather pick my battles, and dealing with the twin dragons later on will be hard enough if Hope is Jabir's true mate. Besides, I think we have a few years before we need to worry about it," he dryly replied.

Paul looked over toward Jabir where he was holding up a large insect for Hope to touch. The awe on her tiny face, reminded him so much of Trisha and Morah. Cree was hovering near the two dragonlings with an expression of uncertainty. Paul sighed and shook his head in sympathy. He remembered his own angst with Trisha when she was younger. All he needed to do was look at Kelan and Bálint to know that everything would be fine. Fortunately, he had a few years before he had to worry about Morah.

"Let's get some firewood before it gets dark," he said.

Later that evening, the large group sat around the fire. Dinner consisted of sandwiches, fresh fruit, and nuts—compliments of a care package from the women. The children finally mellowed out after a day of running around exploring and chasing each other. All but two had reverted to their dragon or tiger cub shape.

Alice and Phoenix sat next to each other. Paul looked around the canopy of trees surrounding them. He didn't miss the fact that Phoenix kept looking up at one tree in particular and smiling. Even Harvey, Creon's symbiot, seemed to sense there was another presence close by.

Do you sense anything? he asked, looking over at his symbiot that was curled up with Morah. Focusing on his dragon, he mentally touched his other half.

Goddesses are near, his dragon replied with a yawn.

Paul frowned. *Is that a good or a bad thing?* he asked.

Goddesses good thing. They like dragonlings, his dragon responded.

"You feel them, too," Creon murmured, glancing warily around them.

"Yes. I don't think we have anything to worry about," Paul replied.

Creon didn't say anything. Paul noticed Creon's eyes were locked on his youngest daughter. Phoenix was giggling and whispering with Alice, Ha'ven and Emma's daughter. Alice waved her hand and the doll in Phoenix's hand changed. Gone was the pale skin, red hair, and green princess dress. The doll now had a dark complexion and was wearing a leather vest, pants, and boots and carrying a bow complete with tiny arrows in a miniature quiver.

A soft chuckle slipped from his lips when Morah suddenly lifted her head and growled at Alice for changing the clothing on her doll. Alice giggled and waved her hand over the doll again, changing the leather clothing to a bright red princess dress complete with appropriate accessories. Morah snorted and nodded in satisfaction.

"Who would like to hear a story?" Paul asked, deciding that no camp-out was complete without a campfire tale.

"I do!" a chorus of young voices called out.

At the word 'story' the children shifted back into their human form. They gathered together to sit in a small group on a log. Paul chuckled when he heard sounds of male groans in the background. He raised an eyebrow when he saw Zoran frantically shaking his head and waving his hands. Paul returned the other man's look with a raised eyebrow.

"Paul, I really don't think that is such a good idea," Zoran started to say when the children—and some of the other men—drowned him out.

"Why?" Paul asked.

"Abby said..." Zoran began, looking around and trying to think of a good way of saying what he had to say without upsetting the children.

Vox leaned over and slapped Zoran on the shoulder. "Probably the same thing that Riley did," Vox teased.

"And Ariel," Mandra added with a grin.

"And Carmen," Creon murmured.

Calo shrugged. "Melina just made Cree and me promise that we would not lose Hope again," he said with a wink at his daughter.

"I think Melina and Emma have been talking," Ha'ven chuckled.

"Please, Dada, I wants a story," Morah pleaded.

"Yes. Please, Grandpa, we want to hear a story," Zohar said, looking up at him with wide imploring eyes.

"Well, if your fathers don't want me to tell you one…," Paul started to say.

"Please, Daddy. I do love stories," Phoenix quietly pleaded, looking at Creon with eyes that swirled with color.

"Okay, but… You kids have to promise us that you understand that this is just a story," Creon cautioned, shooting a warning look at Paul.

The kids squealed and clapped their hands. Even the symbiots perked up, tilting their heads and shimmering with shifting colors to show their excitement. Paul took a breath and thought for a moment. A smile curved his lips when the story came to him. He stood up and focused on the children as he began his story with the same dramatic flair that he'd used when he told Trisha, Ariel, and Carmen stories around the campfires when they were growing up.

"Did you know that there is magic in the woods?" he asked, looking at each of the children.

"Magic? Like this?" Alice asked, fluttering her fingers and causing several large, rainbow-colored butterflies to appear.

Paul chuckled when all the other kids reached for the butterflies that dissolved at their touch, sprinkling them with colorful dust. Ha'ven shrugged his shoulders in apology. Paul waited until the kids settled back down before he continued.

"Very similar to that, Alice, only this magic comes from… the Leprechauns," he said.

"Oh! I love Leprechauns!" Morah announced with a dreamy sigh.

Paul paused when Leo raised his hand. "Yes, Leo?" Paul asked.

"Can I eats them?" the little boy asked with a hopeful grin.

Viper grimaced. "I'm sorry, Paul. Leo wants to eat everything at the moment," he muttered, leaning down and murmuring in his son's ear.

"Oh," Leo sighed, looking disappointed. "I bets they tastes good."

"Continue with your story, Paul, otherwise we might be here all night," Zoran suggested.

"Sorry, Uncle Zoran," Alice and Leo said.

Paul rubbed his chin. "Now, where was I? Oh, yes, the magic in the woods.... Long, long ago, there lived a mighty King. He was the strongest, mightiest King of all the lands," Paul said.

"Just like you, Dad," Zohar said with a proud expression.

"Mine, too," Alice said.

"Mine, two, three, whatever," Roam agreed with a firm nod.

"And my dada," Morah said with a sigh.

"Okay, just like all of them—and me," Paul agreed. "Now, this King lived in a beautiful kingdom and had a strong army, but he had one weakness," he continued before pausing and looking around the group.

"What is it?" Cree finally asked, flushing when everyone turned to look at him for interrupting. "What? I want to know."

"Gold. The King loved gold. Eventually, his hunger for gold would take over his life and his kingdom. The Keeper of the Stories, who was his sister, warned King Tamblin that if he was not careful, his greed would turn his skin green, and his heart would turn cold to all the other things that used to matter to him. But, alas, King Tamblin refused to listen to Tia, his beloved sister," Paul said with a heartfelt sigh.

"Oh, no! What happened, Grandpa?" Bálint asked, sitting forward.

Paul hunkered down and gazed at the children through the low flames. He lowered his voice and looked around him as if he were about to tell them a vital secret. Each of the children leaned forward in anticipation.

"An old man appeared at the castle. He was not just any old man, he was the King of the Leprechauns in disguise. In the pouch at his waist, he carried a single gold coin. The old man explained to King Tamblin that he was simply passing through, and he asked for food and shelter for just a few hours because he still had a long journey before sunrise. At first, King Tamblin was going to turn away the old man, but he caught sight of the pouch and asked the old man what he carried in it. The old man shrugged and told King Tamblin that it was a gold coin, not just any gold coin, but the gold coin of the magical King of the Leprechauns!" Paul exclaimed, standing and throwing his hands out.

Morah clapped her hands together in excitement while the other kids oohed and ahhed. Paul winked at his young daughter because she had heard this story before, but was reacting as if it were the first time.

"What did King Tamblin do?" Ha'ven asked.

"If he is as greedy a bas...." Vox started to say before he cleared his throat. "Ah, if he is as greedy as Paul says, he probably slit the old man's throat and took it."

Roam turned, looked up, and scowled at his dad. "That mean bastard. You'd show him that stealing was wrong, wouldn't you, Dad?" Roam hissed.

"You bet your asssss...ets," Vox started to agree before his brother elbowed him in the side. "Oh, yeah. Roam, remember what Mommy said about your language."

Roam frowned. "I thought she was talking to you. She was waving her finger at you, Dad," Roam said with a confused expression.

"She was, wasn't she?" Vox agreed with a grin that disappeared when Viper shook his head.

"You are going to get us both in trouble if Leo starts repeating things again," Viper warned.

"You gots to be quiets so Dada can finish the story. It's my favorites one!" Morah bossily ordered, turning to shoot Vox and Viper a stern look.

The men sitting around the fire chuckled. "You tell them, Morah," Trelon encouraged. "So, what happened next, Paul?"

"King Tamblin demanded that the old man turn the gold coin over to him, but the old man refused, saying he needed it. The old man was on his way back to the mystical city of the Leprechauns. He must return before the next morning, and the gold coin was his key to entering the city. Now, you need to understand that before he became greedy for gold, King Tamblin had been a wise, noble, and compassionate man, but he was none of those anymore. The hunger for gold had filled his heart with greed, and now he was a very shrewd, devious, and cold-hearted King. At first, King Tamblin demanded the coin as payment for food and shelter, but the old man shook his head.

"'Nay,' the old man said with a wave of his finger. 'I will continue on my journey and sleep along the side of the road.'

"But, Tia, King Tamblin's sister, pleaded with the king.

"'No, brother. You must find it in your heart to give food and shelter,' Tia's soft voice implored on behalf of the old man.

"You see, Tia is not only King Tamblin's sister, but she is the Keeper of the Stories of their people, and she saw the changes in her brother. Tia was as compassionate and loving as her brother, now, was greedy. Tia finally insisted that the old man stay and rest, and her brother agreed. King Tamblin sat moodily at the head of the long table and watched the old man laugh as he shared, with Tia and the knights, the wondrous story of the King of the Leprechauns and the mystical kingdom of Glitter. All were unaware that the old man was testing King Tamblin in the hopes of tricking him." Paul paused again and pointed his finger at his audience. "You see, the old man, tired of living his life confined to being small and living in Glitter, had escaped for one night in the hopes of finding someone else to take his place. The old man saw the sly and devious look in King Tamblin's eyes and knew that his plan was working."

"Smart old man, using his opponent's weakness against him," Ha'ven murmured with an approving nod.

Paul chuckled, enjoying how the men were getting into and analyzing his story. Clearing his throat, he continued.

"While the old Leprechaun King had his own devious plan in motion, so, too, did King Tamblin. Tamblin watched the old man drink many tankards of ale, growing tipsier with each one. Just as he hoped, the old man pulled the pouch from his waist and withdrew the gold coin. The coin was passed around the table until it reached King Tamblin at last. Holding the gold coin in his hand, King Tamblin marveled at the pure beauty of it. Ninety-nine percent pure and as large as the palm of his hand, the coin was embellished with the likeness of the King of the Leprechauns on the front and the Queen of the Wood Fairies on the reverse.

"'Are there more coins such as this?' King Tamblin nonchalantly asked, turning the gold coin over and over in his hand, completely mesmerized by the weight and beauty of it.

"'Mountains of them,' the old man slyly replied. 'The streets are covered with gold, as are the buildings and statues. Each resident of Glitter receives a magical duck that lays a golden egg daily. When the eggs are cracked, the insides contain a nugget of the purest gold in all the universe. They smelt the gold and pour it into molds and make the coins.'"

Paul paused, seeing all the wide eyes focused on him as they drank in his every word. Each time he retold this story, it became bigger and more elaborate than the time before. Taking a deep breath, he continued.

"King Tamblin knew right then and there that he had to find this magical, mystical kingdom and claim it for his own. Once again, he demanded that the old man give him the coin and again the old man refused. Finally, in a fit of rage, he ordered his guards to seize the old man and lock him in the deepest cell in his dungeon. King Tamblin ignored his sister's outcry of horror and the old man's dire warnings that whoever held the gold coin must return it to the kingdom of the Leprechauns by first light or the city and the Little People who lived there would be lost forever. King Tamblin refused to listen to the old man's wild warnings. He was lost in the beauty of the gold coin that he now held in his hand."

Paul grew quiet. He bent down, picked up several sticks, and carefully placed them in the fire. He purposely paused in his tale to let everyone think about what King Tamblin had done. He could sense the tension rising among the group. It wasn't until Calo released an impatient snarl that he knew they were ready for the climax of the story.

"Well, what happened? Did King Tamblin keep the gold coin? What about the old man? What happened to him?" Calo demanded.

"It's okay, Daddy. Everything's goings to be alrights," Hope said, patting her dad on his knee.

Calo's expression grew tender, and he bent down, picked up his daughter, and placed her on his lap. Cree reached over and brushed Hope's dark-brown hair back from her cheek. The love on the two men's faces for the little girl was a tangible reminder that no matter where you lived in the universe, love and family mattered.

"King Tamblin sat at the table in the dining hall long after everyone else retired for the night. The large fire in the hearth burned down to a bed of coals, and still he sat, twirling the gold coin in his hand and rubbing it between his fingers, completely enthralled. Just before dawn, King Tamblin looked at the hearth in surprise when tiny sparks began to dance. Before long, the sparks grew until the vision of a tall, beautiful woman appeared," Paul said.

"A Wood Fairy," Morah breathed with delight.

Paul nodded. "Not just any Wood Fairy, but the Queen of the Wood Fairies. She knew who the old man was and what he was planning, for to reach King Tamblin's kingdom, he'd had to pass through her forest. She also knew that she wouldn't let the Kingdom of Glitter or the Little People perish. Throughout the night, the Queen of the Wood Fairies had watched from the hearth as King Tamblin stared, mesmerized, at the gold in his hand. Stepping toward him, she searched his tired face," Paul said, staring down at the dancing flames in the fire pit.

"*'Why do you keep the gold coin?'* the Queen of the Wood Fairies asked solemnly.

"King Tamblin looked up at the Queen of the Wood Fairies with dazed eyes. *'It calls to me,'* King Tamblin admitted. *'I see a city that glitters when I look at the gold and feel the warmth of the metal flowing through my soul,'* the King said, peering back at the Queen of the Wood Fairies with an unhealthy hunger in his eyes.

"*'You wish to go to the city that glitters?'* the Queen asked.

"*'More than anything,'* King Tamblin replied.

"*'Give to me the gold coin, and I will make your wish come true, King Tamblin,'* the Queen instructed with a graceful bow of her head. She held out her hand.

"King Tamblin gripped the gold coin in his hand. At first, he was reluctant to part with it, but the more he thought about what the old man had said, the more he wanted to have *all* the gold and not just a single coin. He reluctantly placed the coin in the Queen's hand and made his wish.

"*'I wish to go to the Kingdom of Glitter,'* King Tamblin stated.

"*'Sleep, King Tamblin, and when you wake, your wish will have come true. But be warned, you will never be able to return to your kingdom here unless you first do four things. First, you must give up your greed for gold. This will only happen when you find something more precious to warm your heart. Second, only the bravest of all warriors can return the gold coin to you. You must be willing to give the coin to one who will hold it dear to their heart. Only then will you truly become King of, not just the Leprechauns, but also the people of Glitter. Third, you must understand that to be strong, you must at times be humble. Finally, only when you are given a gift that is rare, magical, and untouched by greed, will you finally understand what it means to be home—for home is truly where the heart is, King Tamblin, and that is far more precious than all the gold in the world,'* the Queen of the Wood Fairies warned."

Paul looked around the group. "King Tamblin closed his eyes and fell into a deep sleep. When he woke the next morning, he was no longer in his own kingdom. He was now in the Kingdom of Glitter, but that was not all.

"Lest you forgot, when Tamblin took the gold coin, it belonged to none other than the King of the Leprechauns. Now, Tamblin had traded the coin for a wish, but he still held the power of the Leprechaun's gold in his cold heart. He would be the new King of the Leprechauns and ruler of the Little People of Glitter but, as a reminder of the greed in his heart, the Queen of the Wood Fairies had turned King Tamblin's skin green.

"As the years passed, King Tamblin soon grew to love and respect the people of Glitter, but he also missed his sister. King Tamblin saw that while the citizens of Glitter had as much gold as they wanted, that was not what made them happy. Their love for each other is what warmed their hearts.

"Over time, the dazzle of gold did not call to King Tamblin the way it once had. Instead, he longed for the sound of his sister's voice and the wisdom of her stories.

"So, he began looking for the four things the Queen of the Wood Fairies had instructed him to find in the hopes of bringing her to Glitter.

"Each year in March, a doorway would open along the boundary of his kingdom for one single night. In preparation to make the doorway connect to his former kingdom, King Tamblin searched for the bravest warriors who would help him recover the gold coin from the Queen of the Wood Fairies. However, he still needed one bit of magic to make it all work," Paul said, pausing again.

"But... What is the magic he needs?" Creon asked.

"I knows!" Morah said, twirling to face her uncle. "A four-leaf clover! You gets four wishes with it, but you gots to be careful what's you wishes for."

"I have a question. What is a four-leaf clover?" Kelan asked with a frown.

CHAPTER FOUR

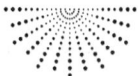

"That was a great story, Paul," Mandra said an hour later.

Paul chuckled. He looked over at where Morah lay tucked under the blanket in their makeshift shelter. The soft and reassuring snores of the kids could be heard coming from the various covered sleeping areas. He looked up as Creon and Trelon approached the fire. Both men looked worn out.

"Did you find them?" Paul asked with a raised eyebrow.

"Yeah, finally," Trelon said with a yawn. He scratched his stomach. "At least the girls didn't bring anything too destructive with them."

Creon held up his hand. Even in the dim light of the fire, it was obvious something had bitten his hand several times. A wry smile twisted his lips.

"So says the warrior who refused to stick his hand in the hole," Creon muttered.

Trelon shook his head. "First of all, it was your daughter who dug the hole, not mine. Second, I warned you that you might want to ask Harvey to take a look first. Hell, I even offered to ask Symba," he retorted, motioning to his symbiot who now formed a nice thick bed and a large tent.

"You know that is cheating, right?" Mandra asked, looking at the shelter Trelon's symbiot formed.

Trelon shook his head and grinned. "You're just jealous I thought of using Symba. Besides, with Amber and Jade, I need all the help I can get. They are getting even more creative as they get older."

"What did they build this time that has teeth?" Paul asked, nodding toward Creon's hand.

"Well, after I finally found the hole Spring dug for her and Phoenix to sleep in, I discovered that Amber and Jade had joined them. What Trelon neglected to tell me was that his two had been working on a new defense bot," Creon dryly replied.

"A defense bot?" Mandra asked with a raised eyebrow.

"Think replicas of the girls in their dragon forms with lots of very sharp teeth," Creon explained.

Trelon chuckled. "I thought it was very innovative of them to make tiny robots of themselves in their dragon forms," he said with a grin.

"Almost as innovative as Paul when he included those species that Ariel discovered on that moon in his story. At least we won't have to worry about the kids going on an adventure to find them!" Mandra commented.

Paul shrugged. "When you and Ariel shared the story with us, I knew Morah would get a kick out of it. I just added a little Irish mythology to the story, threw in a hint of a holiday we have back on Earth called St. Patrick's Day, and the whole thing made for the perfect bedtime tale. Morah reminds me so much of Trisha, Ariel, and Carmen at that age. They loved it when I made up stories," he said.

"Well, I don't know about you, but watching the girls on my own is worse than training new warriors. I'm exhausted," Trelon said behind a yawn before he stood up and stretched.

Mandra looked at the hard ground and thin blanket in his shelter. He brushed his hand over the symbiot on his wrist. Jabir was already sound asleep on Precious. In seconds, the symbiot had carefully transformed under the little boy to create a shelter identical to the one Symba created for Trelon.

Paul chuckled when he saw Zoran, Mandra, and Kelan's symbiots do the same thing. Not to be outdone, Ha'ven waved his hand and created an elaborate tent for him and Alice. Vox, Viper, and the two cubs had disappeared earlier. Paul suspected they were comfortably ensconced in a tree somewhere.

With a sigh, he brushed the symbiot on his wrist. He decided there really wasn't any reason not to take advantage of having a little comfort. After all, it wasn't like this was a boot camp for survival training. It was a family camp-out.

"Good night. I'll see you in the morning," Paul quietly said before retreating to his and Morah's now very comfortable shelter.

He kneeled down next to Morah and picked up the half-dozen dolls scattered across his side of the bed. He piled them on the ground beside her before lying down. He lifted his arm when a thin blanket formed over him.

"Thank you, Crash," Paul murmured with a contented sigh. "Help me keep an eye on her."

Warmth filled him. For a brief moment, he remembered that he was going to check to see if the Goddesses were still hanging around. No sooner had that thought flashed through his mind than sleep pulled at him. The last thing he thought about was that he hoped they'd enjoyed the story as much as the children and guys did, if they even stayed to listen to it.

Arosa sighed as she watched all the children and men slowly settle down for the night. Arilla floated down to sit next to her in the tree.

Her sister wiggled her golden nose when one of the smaller symbiots stuck its head out of a tent. A moment later, Morah atop Princess Buttercup approached them. She carefully slid to the ground and turned to look up at her.

"Come, sister," Arosa murmured, floating down to sit on one of the logs.

Arilla joined her sister down on the logs that encircled the rock-lined firepit. With a wave of her hand, the flames rose from the bed of coals. The campsite was cast in soft, shadowed hues. Arosa solidified and opened her arms to the little girl when she toddled toward her, rubbing her sleepy eyes.

"I saw you," Morah said with a wide yawn as she climbed up onto Arosa's lap and snuggled against her. "Mommy says I goings to be likes her. Are you's Princess Buttercup's mommies?"

Arosa looked over Morah's head and chuckled. That was what these two goddesses loved about this species. They never knew what was going to happen or what they would say or do. There was always an adventure waiting to unfold with these little ones.

"Yes, I guess we are Princess Buttercup's mothers," Arosa replied.

"Did you like Dada's story? He's the bestest storytellers in the whole world," Morah bragged with a sigh.

"Yes, it was a wonderful story," Arilla agreed, touching Morah's soft, curly hair.

"I wishes...," Morah started to say before a yawn stopped her and she closed her eyes.

Arosa gently stroked her hand down Morah's back as she held her. She was curious about the little girl's wish. Arilla looked at her with questioning eyes as well.

"What do you wish for, little Priestess?" Arilla gently asked.

"I wishes the story was trues. I wants to meets a real live Leprechaun," Morah answered before lifting her hand and sliding her thumb in her mouth.

Arilla looked at her sister with a mischievous grin. Arosa started to shake her head. Usually, she was the one who made the impulsive decisions that got them into trouble with the elder of their species, Aikaterina.

"Sleep, little Priestess. When you wake, your wish will be granted. Oh, and look for the magic four-leaf clover," Arilla murmured, remembering that part of the story.

Arosa stood up with Morah in her arms and floated over to her symbiot tent. The fluid body of the symbiot parted at her silent command and Arosa laid Morah down next to her father. Rising upward, the symbiot covered the father and daughter once again with Princess Buttercup resuming her place next to Morah.

Arosa's body shimmered and faded. She looked at her sister and laughed. What harm could there be in granting Morah's wish? With a whisper, both sisters waved their hands. Power swirled through the air, wrapping around each of the men sleeping in the tents. At the same time, a portal to a beautiful kingdom opened—a kingdom with a city that glittered and was ruled by none other than the unsuspecting King of the Leprechauns, King Tamblin.

CHAPTER FIVE

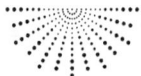

"*W*here's my daddy?" Jabir asked early the next morning, looking around and scratching his belly as Precious sniffed the ground where they had been sleeping.

"I don't know. We can't find our daddy either. And I don't remember this place. The trees look all funny," Amber and Jade said, bounding up to the other children.

"I can't find my dad either," Roam complained, shifting from his tiger cub and looking around at the colorful forest with a puzzled expression. "I've sniffed everywhere and Bálint said he couldn't find no tracks."

A slight sniffle escaped Hope and she looked around with wide, frightened eyes. Phoenix and Alice immediately stepped closer to the tiny little girl. Leo sniffed the air before he sneezed. Shifting from a black tiger cub back into a little boy, he shook his head.

"I don't smells nothing eithers and I don't sees no blood. I don't thinks they gots eaten. There would be lots of blood if they's gots eaten and pieces of thems all overs the place," Leo said, pawing at the dew-damp soil.

Zohar rolled his eyes and shook his head at the younger boy. He looked around at the unusual forest. This was not the same one they were in yesterday. The trees here weren't much taller than their dads, and mixed throughout them were mushrooms in a variety of shapes, sizes, and colors that were large enough to stand underneath them. Gone were the huge trees and thick ferns they played in yesterday. Also gone were the fire pit and circle of logs that they sat around last night.

He had woken up when he felt Goldie, his parents' symbiot, shake him. Zohar hadn't been too concerned when he saw that his dad was gone—until he couldn't find him. That was when he had woken Bálint and Roam. Soon, their whispers had woken the others. As each youngling emerged from their tents, they all said the same thing—their dads were missing. As the oldest and the son of the King of the Valdier, Zohar decided he would have to take charge.

"I think we need to spread out and look for them. Phoenix, Alice, and Spring stay close to Hope. Amber, you and Jade take to the trees. Jabir, you talk to any animals you can find and see if they saw what happened. Bálint, I need you to find some tracks," Zohar ordered, turning to each dragonling as he spoke.

"What do you want us to do, Zohar?" Roam asked, looking at the other boy.

Zohar looked over at Leo who had shifted back into a cub again and grimaced. Roam's cousin had the wings of an insect hanging out of his mouth, and it looked like he had another bug trapped beneath one of his front paws. Nodding his head at Leo, he hoped Roam understood what he was trying to tell him.

"Search the camp for any clues and make sure Leo doesn't eat them," Zohar instructed before he paused and looked around. "Where's Morah?" he suddenly asked.

Everyone turned toward the tent Grandpa Paul and Morah had slept in. Morah, hearing her name, sat up and rubbed her eyes. Realizing that she was the only one in the tent, she clumsily climbed out and motioned for Crash to reform into the shape of a unicorn while Princess Buttercup took on the shape of a jackrabbit from her father's world, complete with extra-long ears and fluffy tail.

Zohar hurried over to where she stood rubbing her eyes again. She yawned and stretched, her bare toes peeking out from under her long, red princess gown. She blinked up at him when he stopped in front of her.

"Do you know where Grandpa is?" Zohar anxiously asked.

Zohar saw the confusion on her face. She thought about what he said for a moment before she turned and looked at where Crash was rubbing his nose against the soft blue-green grass. Zohar watched her tilt her head and look around her with an expression of wonder on her face, turning in a circle until she was facing him once again. She shook her head.

"Nope, I haven't seen Dada since I wents to sleep after I talks to the Goddesses," Morah replied with a frown.

"You saw the Goddesses?" Alice asked, stepping closer to Morah.

"I saw them last night, but I was sleepy," Phoenix said, looking at Morah. "I thought they were just listening to Grandpa's story. They like our story-time."

Morah looked at the kids with an expression of uncertainty on her face and nodded. "They liked Dada's story and…," she paused and looked over at Zohar.

"And what?" Zohar encouraged.

Morah smoothed her red princess dress with her hands and bit her lip. She frowned and looked down at the ground. Zohar could tell that she was trying to remember something from the way she was mumbling to herself. She suddenly looked up at him with a troubled expression.

"The Goddesses was going to give me my wishes. I's suppose to looks for the… for the… I can't remembers what its called," she said in an uncertain tone. "My dada would know." Her little voice quavered.

Zohar took a step closer to Morah and looked down at her. "What did you wish for?" he asked.

Morah looked up at Zohar. "I wish to goes to Glitter to sees the Leprechauns," she said.

"Do you think...?" Alice started to say, her lips parting in wonder.

"What if...?" Phoenix said at the same time.

A soft growl drew their attention. Zohar bit back a laugh when he saw Roam looking at his cousin. Leo was tugging on the stem of a large-leafed plant before it snapped off.

Roam grabbed one of the leafy parts of the plant and yanked on it. "Leo, spit it out! Your mommy said you aren't supposed to eat stuff without asking permission first," Roam growled, tugging on a large, oddly shaped leaf.

Leo suddenly opened his mouth and spit out the stem. Roam fell backwards onto the ground, the bright green leaf between his hands. The small, black tiger cub made a face and wiped at his tongue with his front paw. It was obvious that he didn't care for the taste of the plant.

"Wait, look at that! It has four leaves, just like the plant Grandpa told us about," Spring exclaimed, hurrying over to where he was now sitting on the soft grass.

The kids gathered around her and Roam. Zohar watched Spring take the leaf from Roam and turn it over. Brilliant lights of glittering green danced along the veins of each of the four curved leaves.

"Oh, it is so pretty," Alice said, studying the dancing lights with delight.

Spring dropped the stem when a shape suddenly appeared in the center of it. They all stared in awe at the image of a beautiful woman with four small transparent wings. The woman's long hair was the colors of the flames from last night's fire. Around her head, she wore a crown of green with tiny white flowers and dark red berries growing on it.

"Oh, she's gots a princess dress on," Morah breathed, stepping forward to run her fingers through the image.

The woman's long, many layered gown was a mixture of colors varying from a dark golden-yellow to red, orange, and green. The woman floated above the center of the plant and turned in a circle. On her face was a soft, compassionate smile.

"Who is she?" Amber asked, reaching out to touch the woman as well.

Morah's lips parted in a small gasp, and her eyes widened. "I knows who she is! She is the Queen of the Wood Fairies!" she breathed in awe.

"But… I thoughts she was makeups," Hope whispered.

Morah shook her head. "The Goddesses tolds me last night that my wishes will come trues when I wakes up. I am supposes to finds a four-leaf clover. It's gots magic."

Alice reached out and touched the edge of the leaf. She drew in a startled breath and pulled back her hand against her chest. Her eyes were wide with uncertainty.

"Did it hurt you?" Bálint demanded, reaching for her hand.

Alice shook her head. "No, but it has lots of energy in it," she said. "I wish my daddy was here. He'd know what to do."

Zohar glanced around the unusual forest again. He wished his dad was there, too. His lips tightened in determination. Looking at the translucent image hovering above the center of the plant, he bent over and picked up the clover.

"If the Queen of the Wood Fairies is here, then maybe the King of the Leprechauns is too. Grandpa said that the King needed warriors to help him. Our dads are the best warriors ever!" Zohar stated, holding the clover's stem tightly in his fist.

"But… How are we going to find them?" Jade asked.

"It's alls my fault," Morah whispered, her voice quivering with tears. "I makes a wish to meets a real-live leprechaun and nows he tooks all our daddies."

"It's okay, Morah. We'll save our dads, won't we?" Zohar asked, looking at the other kids.

"Yes!" all the other kids said.

Zohar watched the girls gather around Morah. Amber wrapped her arms around Morah and hugged her. The little girl sniffed before she wiped the tears from her face and lifted her chin.

"I promises my mommy that I wouldn't let nothings happen to Dada. I's going to finds the King of the Leprechauns and tells him to give him back," Morah announced, stepping forward and taking the clover from Zohar's hand.

"I's going to go gets both of my daddies back, too," Hope said, her eyes brimming with tears and determination.

"What are we going to do, Zohar?" Spring asked, looking at him.

"The four-leaf clover," Alice suddenly said. "Can't we make a wish on it?"

Phoenix eagerly nodded. "We should get four wishes," she said with wide eyes.

"But, I thoughts only the King of the Leprechauns could makes wish-es," Hope said.

Amber touched the smallest leaf. "Well, I think it's worth a try," she said before turning to look at her sister. "Jade, do you have our secret weapons?"

Jade smiled, turned to show the backpack on her back, and nodded. "Yep! I'm ready," she announced.

"What about the symbiots? Mommy said I was to have my symbiot and Precious with me at all times—just in case Daddy loses me," Jabir said with a sheepish expression.

Zohar thought for a moment. "We'll make a circle. As long as we're touching each other, we should all be able to make the wish," he said, waving to everyone to gather around. "Everyone, hold hands and don't forgets your symbiots! Morah, since you were the one that made the first wish, I think you should make this one, too."

Morah swallowed. "I wishes to find the Leprechauns," she said in a loud, clear voice.

They all waited, but nothing happened. Frowning, Zohar looked around. He softly counted each of the dragonlings, Alice, Roam, and....

His eyes widened in alarm. "Where's Leo?" Zohar asked in exasperation.

CHAPTER SIX

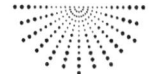

*P*aul knew the moment he woke that something was wrong —very, very wrong. He looked up at the glittering rock surface and blinked. He should have been looking up at the ceiling of a symbiot-created tent, or at the very least, the canopy of the massive branches and leaves of the surrounding forest. Sitting up, he cautiously looked around before rising to his feet.

He rotated in a tight circle, examining his surroundings. Brightly colored mushrooms in many hues greeted his stunned eyes. If waking to find himself in a cave surrounded by a mushroom forest wasn't shocking enough, the fact that the mushrooms were ten times as tall as he was made him reach down to pinch his arm to make sure he wasn't still dreaming.

A flash of pain confirmed what he dreaded—this was real. He looked around, spying the other men still asleep. What concerned him the most was what was missing.

"Morah," Paul called softly, searching the area for his tiny daughter.

He spied something shimmering on the ground where he had awakened. Retracing his steps, he bent down and picked up the half-buried gold coin. Turning it over in the palm of his hand, he noticed that on one side was the picture of a man and on the other side of that a beautiful wood fairy. Disbelief warred with reality.

He looked up and turned when he saw a movement out of the corner of his eye. Zoran was staring at him with a confused frown. Paul pocketed the coin and motioned Zoran to wake the others. He silently walked over to Vox and Viper where they lay sleeping. Kneeling on one knee between them, he shook each man.

"Wake up. We've got trouble," Paul quietly instructed.

Vox and Viper immediately came awake and rolled until they were crouching next to him. Their expressions were alert and wary at the same time. Viper shifted into his black tiger form.

"Where the hell are we?" Vox hissed, studying the surrounding terrain.

Paul shook his head. "I don't know, but the kids and our symbiots aren't here," he said in a grim voice.

"Spread out and search the immediate area," Zoran ordered.

Paul rose to his feet and silently moved out among the mushrooms. He noticed that Vox had shifted into his leopard form, also. Reaching inside himself, he touched his dragon. Shock ran through him when he discovered his dragon was still sleeping.

Wake up. I could use a little assistance, Paul ordered.

A vision of his dragon raising his head, sniffing, and lying back down came to him. If he didn't know any better, he'd think the damn thing was about to go back to sleep. He issued another silent order to help.

It the Goddesses. All your fault, his dragon replied with a yawn.

All my fault? How in the hell is this my fault?! Paul growled, pausing under a large mushroom.

"Paul!" Zoran suddenly hissed.

"*Dragon's balls*! Not again," Creon groaned.

"Ariel is going to kill me," Mandra muttered.

Cree turned and glared over at Paul. "Ariel?! Melina is going to castrate Calo and me. We swore that we wouldn't lose Hope again!" he snapped.

The sound of his dragon snickering told Paul that the other dragons had come to the same conclusion—the Goddesses were up to their usual mischief, and they were all on another adventure. However, that still didn't tell him if the kids were safe or where in the hell they were! A little forewarning would have come in handy.

Dragonlings have symbiots and each other. They fine, his dragon replied with glee.

"Well, do you know where in the hell we are?" he demanded out loud to his dragon, putting his hands on his hips in frustration.

Vox shifted into his two-legged form and turned to glare at him. "How in the hell are we supposed to know if you don't?" Vox snapped, walking toward him.

Viper shifted as well. Paul warily watched as all the men gathered around him. Kelan and Trelon didn't say anything—they didn't have to. They were the only two who didn't look as if they wanted to string him up.

"What do you two think is so amusing?" Ha'ven asked, crossing his arms and looking at the two men with a glare and a raised eyebrow.

Kelan shook his head. "I'm just glad the women aren't here. We'd never live this down if they were," he chuckled.

A reluctant smile of amusement pulled at the corner of Ha'ven's lips. Paul lifted his hand and ran it over the back of his neck. An image of Morian's beautiful face flashed through his mind, and he shook his head.

Yes, I can see her laughing as well, he thought in resignation to his dragon, who happened to be enjoying this far too much for his liking.

Paul looked up when he saw Cree and Calo reappear from out of the mushroom forest. They had left an hour before to do a short reconnaissance of the area. Both men had streaks of red, blue, yellow, and orange on their hair and clothing.

"We don't recognize any of this," Cree said with a shake of his head.

"We did find a trail through the mushrooms leading that way. I've never seen anything like this on Valdier," Calo replied.

Paul's eyes paused on Mandra. The man looked like he wanted to say something but wasn't quite sure how to phrase it. At this point, Paul decided that spitting out any possible scenarios was the optimal choice. It wouldn't be that difficult to eliminate them from the list.

"What is it, Mandra?" Paul prodded.

Mandra looked over at the mushroom forest behind Cree and Calo before he turned his uneasy glance on Paul.

"This place looks a lot like the one Ariel told us about, the one you mentioned in your story, but that is impossible," he said with a shake of his head.

Zoran frowned. "Well, it is obvious we are not on Valdier. Where else could we be?" he asked.

"I don't know about the rest of you, but I'm of the opinion that not being on Valdier is the least of our worries. Am I the only one who has noticed that we are surrounded by giant mushrooms?" Ha'ven queried.

"So, what? We've seen lots of unusual plant life on other planets before," Vox said, running his hand down the stem of the mushroom he was standing beside.

Ha'ven turned and looked at Vox with a raised eyebrow. "Have you seen anything like this before? Personally, I've never seen a mushroom that was larger than my fist on any planet that I've been on. Have you?" he inquired.

Vox warily looked around the forest of mushrooms and shook his head. "No, not a mushroom," he agreed.

"So, what are we supposed to do, oh, mighty teller of tales?" Viper sarcastically asked Paul. "If Vox and I don't find our sons, Riley and Tina are going to be the least of our concerns," he added, glancing at his brother with a pained expression before turning back to look at Paul.

"Oh, Goddess. If Riley doesn't kill me, Pearl will. And, I promise you, she'll enjoy prolonging it," Vox groaned, lifting his hands and running them over his face.

Viper nodded. "Pearl and Tina both will have my head. Plus, I have to find Leo. I swear that boy isn't safe to leave on his own. If he isn't trying to eat everything, he is disappearing," he warned with a shake of his head.

"Have any of you tried to connect with them through your symbiots?" Ha'ven asked.

Paul briefly closed his eyes at the stunned silence. Of course they hadn't. That would have been the logical thing to do. Shaking his head, he ignored Ha'ven, Vox, and Viper's loud sighs of exasperation when he and the rest of the dragon warriors touched the thin links of gold around their wrists.

He immediately got a brief flash of Morah, her eyes blazing with determination, her little chin lifted in the air, and she was sitting on Crash who was in the shape of a unicorn. He'd seen that look one too many times when he'd tried to convince her to do something she didn't want to do—like wearing pants instead of a princess dress to go camping. A rueful smile curved his lips. He looked around at the other men and saw the same expression. It looked as if the kids were preparing for another adventure.

"Ha'ven, can you do your teleport thing to the kids?" Creon asked, turning to look at his friend.

Ha'ven shook his head. "I already tried. I don't know if it is the cave, something the Goddesses did, or my uncomfortable feeling that things seem much larger than they should, but I appear to have limited abilities at the moment," he reluctantly shared.

"Wow!" Kelan muttered with a soft whistle.

Vox and Viper suddenly hissed and turned. Paul watched the two Sarafin warriors shift into their cat forms in the blink of an eye. He connected with his dragon, but all it was doing was purring with delight.

"What is it?" Paul asked, searching the mushroom forest for anything that could have caused the brothers to go on alert.

Zoran, Kelan, and Trelon were standing next to each other with their heads tilted back and their eyes closed. Each was emitting a soft rumbling that sounded suspiciously like his dragon did. Rubbing his chest, Paul couldn't figure out what was going on.

He looked over at Creon who had shifted to his dragon form. The difference between Creon's dragon with his tail up in the air and an almost devilish gleam in his eyes compared to the uneasy hissing of Vox and Viper added to his confusion. Only Mandra looked wary.

"Mandra, what is it?" Paul asked again.

Ha'ven took a step closer to Mandra and nodded. Paul could feel the Curizan's unease building as well. The man's hands flexed as if he was testing the energy around them.

"I'd like to know as well, if you don't mind sharing," Ha'ven said, hearing movement through the mushrooms.

Mandra's wary eyes remained locked on the direction of the sound that was growing closer. Paul saw the huge warrior swallow.

Suddenly a monstrous brown and white furry creature with beady black eyes, a matching nose, and two very long, sharp teeth rose above the mushrooms in front of them, and they all stumbled back several steps.

"Tasiers!" Mandra muttered, stumbling back and grabbing for Zoran and Kelan.

Paul's eyes widened, and he stared in horror at the massive creature eyeing them. Tasiers! This was the tiny fur-ball that the dragons thought tasted like chocolate? He realized that Ha'ven was right, that something else was very, very wrong at the same time as Ha'ven, Vox, and Viper did.

"Run!" Mandra yelled, turning with his brothers when a half dozen more Tasiers appeared behind the first one.

CHAPTER SEVEN

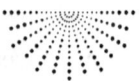

"Are you sure this is the right way, Morah?" Zohar asked, guiding Goldie closer to the little girl riding in the front.

Morah nodded. "Yes, I's sure," she stated with confidence.

Zohar and the others had quickly learned that the magic clover only responded to Morah. It sparkled and turned in the direction they were supposed to go only when she held it. He originally started to lead the group after taking the clover from Morah, but the clover wilted and didn't sparkle as brightly. When he handed it back to Morah, it had perked up and began directing her.

Zohar watched as Bálint, Amber, and Jade rode up on their parents' symbiots while their own small symbiots flew next to them. The three were scouting the area. They reined in their symbiots, each in a different form, and came to a stop when they were close to where he and Morah had halted. The other children gathered around them to hear what they had discovered.

"The forest grows thinner and changes into a sea of sand. I've never seen anything like it before," Bálint said with a worried frown.

"Did you see any tracks?" Zohar asked.

Bálint nodded and leaned forward to run his hand along Bio's neck. The symbiot shimmered at the boy's caress. Zohar motioned for Bálint to tell him what they had seen.

"I saw Leo's tracks. He was chasing something across the sand. There were some strange tracks in the sand near the edge of the forest. It looked like worm tracks but with lots of legs, and they kept disappearing. I think they went under the sand. If it is worms, they made Bio and Symba nervous. They kept pawing at the sand and hopping around," Bálint shared.

"Momma and Aunt Tina are going to be upset if Leo gets eaten," Roam groaned from where he was sitting behind Jabir on Precious.

"Do we have to go that way?" Phoenix asked, circling around on Harvey.

She and her sister, Spring, rode on Harvey, their parents' symbiot, who was in the shape of a large dog with floppy ears.

"Yes, we's got to goes that way," Morah stated, touching her heels to Crash's sides and moving forward.

"When did she get so bossy?" Spring asked with surprise, watching Morah ride ahead.

"I don't know, but she's almost as bossy as Zohar," Bálint observed with a grin.

Zohar shot his cousin a scowl. "Leaders are supposed to be bossy," he declared with a lift of his chin.

"I thoughts only mommies were bossy. That's what my daddy said. I'm gonna have to tell him that Mommy really is the leader, then," Roam said with a confused expression.

Spring and Phoenix looked at each other and giggled. Zohar shook his head. He decided being the leader was a lot harder work than it looked like when his dad did it.

"Let's go before we lose Morah, too," Zohar said, urging Goldie to move on down the trail.

Leo shook the sand off of his paw and growled. He looked around at the rippling granules, and his small, black rounded ears moved like a radar dish searching for a signal. His dark brown eyes lit up when he saw the movement under the sand.

He'd been chasing, catching, and releasing the worms for the past hour. They were fun because they popped up out of the sand. He'd caught ten of them so far. He just had to be careful because they had a mouth with lots of little teeth. They couldn't bite him through his thick fur, but they were hard to shake off.

"Grrr!" he growled, crouching down until his butt was in the air and his tail flicked back and forth.

He was about to pounce when he saw another movement out of the corner of his eye. He raised his head and blinked. These were different creatures. They looked like Morah's dolls only they were dressed like his daddy and the other warriors.

His eyes widened when one of the worms suddenly popped up out of the sand and grabbed a wing on the skimmer that a tall warrior was riding. The force of the worm's attack knocked the warrior off of the small machine. Leo heard shouts of warning at the same time as the sand began to move near the tall warrior.

With a powerful leap, Leo landed close to the man at the exact moment the worm appeared. With a flick of his paw, he sent the worm flying. Crouching down on the sand, he cupped the little doll-like warrior between his paws and loudly hissed at the worm.

His eyes widened in pain when he felt a sharp prick on his right paw. Shifting back to his two-legged form, he started crying.

"Ouchy! That hurts!" Leo sniffed, sucking on his finger and glaring down at the toy warrior. "I's protectings you from the worms. Why's you wants to hurts me?"

The warrior looked up at him in shock. The man glanced at the sword in his hand before he returned it to his scabbard. With a formal bow, he introduced himself before he straightened.

"Please accept my sincere apologies, young warrior. My name is Jett. Who might you be?" Jett asked.

Leo looked warily at the man. Bending down until he was eye level with him, he sniffed him. The toy warrior didn't smell like Morah's toys.

"I's Leo. I's a prince causes my daddy's a prince. Are you reals?" Leo asked.

Jett chuckled. "Yes, I am very real. Where is your father?" Jett asked, searching around the sand dunes.

"I don't knows. Daddy's lost. I's the one that mostly does that. I likes lookings for things," Leo explained.

"Your Majesty, the sand worms," another warrior gently reminded Jett.

"I's Leo. I's a cat-shifter," Leo said with a sharp-toothed grin that had the warrior backing his winged skimmer away from him. "Are you's real too?"

"This is Santil. We were on patrol when we saw your tail and came to investigate," Jett explained.

"I's playing with the worms. They's fun to catch," Leo replied with a grin. "Do you wants me to shows you how to catches them?"

Jett chuckled. "No, I think I will leave the catching of the sand worms to you. We were about to return to Sandora. Perhaps we could be of assistance in finding your father," he offered.

"I's hungry. Do you has anys food? The worms don't tastes good," Leo said with a sigh as his stomach growled. "I's starving."

"I hope he doesn't think we are food," Santil muttered.

Leo giggled and looked at Santil. "Does you tastes good?" he asked.

Jett chuckled. "He tastes *very* good," he said with a wink.

Santil's mouth dropped open, and he shot Jett a panicked look. Leo giggled. Shaking his head, he sat back up.

"That's means you don't tastes very good. My mommy always says it tastes good and winks at my daddy when somethings tastes bad. I's not going to eats you," Leo announced.

"Thank the Goddess for that," Santil muttered.

"If you follow us, young Prince Leo, we will guide you to the Kingdom of the Sand People," Jett replied with a bow.

Leo watched as Jett returned to his winged skimmer and climbed onto it. Delight filled his eyes when he saw it rise above the sands and turn. This was much more fun than playing with sand worms he decided as he shifted back into his tiger form and took off after the flying toy warriors.

CHAPTER EIGHT

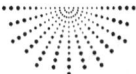

"I think we've lost them," Paul said, drawing in deep, calming breaths and shaking his head in bewilderment. "Would one of you please tell me what in the hell is going on?"

"Those... were Tasiers," Mandra said, leaning his head against the stem of a mushroom.

"I know they were Tasiers, but I thought Tasiers were about this big," Paul growled, holding his hands in a circle the size of a large piece of fruit. "In case I was the only one having a delusional episode, those... creatures were considerably larger than they should be, correct?"

"They were definitely not like any Tasiers I've ever seen before, but they sure did smell like them," Trelon said, rubbing his stomach. "I'm hungry."

Viper shot Trelon an exasperated glance. "Now you sound just like Leo," he said as he slid down to the ground, groaning. "I think the women were right, no more tales—ever!"

Paul watched as Ha'ven turned from where he was keeping a wary look-out behind them. Ha'ven frowned when he started counting heads. Turning all the way around, Ha'ven searched the group.

"Where is Vox... and Kelan?" Ha'ven asked.

"And the twin dragons," Zoran added with a soft curse. "Spread out, we need to find them."

"Goddess, I hope they weren't eaten," Creon groaned, rising from where he was sitting on a small blue and yellow mushroom.

"I don't think spreading out is such a good idea," Viper muttered, slowly rising to his feet.

"Why not...?" Zoran started to ask before his voice faded.

They slowly raised their hands when male and female warriors moved out from behind the mushrooms to surround them. Each of their long staffs was tipped with glowing, pointed red gems, and was held at the ready. Paul was surprised by the color of their skin and the curved shape of their ears that ended in a point at the tips.

"Well, I can honestly say I think I know where we are now," Mandra replied.

Looking up, Paul noticed more warriors riding dozens of bat-like creatures.

"Leprechauns?" he breathed in disbelief.

"I told you they were real," Mandra muttered under his breath.

Paul clamped his mouth shut when the warriors simultaneously pointed their staffs at the group. Now that he had an up close and personal look at the gems, he recognized them as the same ones they had used to defeat Raffvin. He quickly realized that he and the others were in trouble—yet, at the same time, he couldn't help but admire the warriors' successfully stealthy approach.

A tall, slender woman stepped forward. She eyed each of them with a suspicious expression before she addressed them.

"You will come with us. Do not try to resist," the woman ordered.

Paul kept a wary eye on the warriors surrounding them as they motioned for the men to fall into formation and move out. He moved his gaze over the warriors flying overhead again.

As the men followed the line of warriors further down the path, Paul reached up and traced his hand under the gills of a mushroom. The smooth, silky texture ran across his hand.

I don't know if we've ended up on the other side of the rainbow or in one of Jonathan Swift's islands of little people, he thought in disbelief.

It suddenly dawned on him that if they were in the latter, then they had shrunk! A shiver of unease ran through him at the possibility. There was no logical or scientific explanation for what was happening.

The only thing that gave him some peace of mind was the knowledge that the symbiots were with the kids. He knew that Crash and Princess Buttercup would do everything in their considerable power to protect Morah. He only wished that he was there for his daughter. He could only imagine how scared she and the other children had to be.

CHAPTER NINE

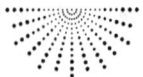

"You's a bad worm. Bad, bad, bad worm! You don't tries to eats my symbiot," Morah snapped, thumping the worm on the head with her small star-tipped wand. "Jabir, tells them all to goes home before I has Crash stomp on them!"

Jabir carefully pulled the sand worm free from where it was hanging onto the symbiot's rabbit tail. He held the worm firmly in his hand and shook his head. Looking up at Morah, he gave her an apologetic smile.

"I don't know how to speak sand worm. Hopefully, they will know enough to leaves us alone," he said, placing the sand worm on the ground and watching it quickly disappear beneath the soft granules.

"Bálint, has you and Roam found Leo yets?" Morah asked, turning on her golden saddle.

"We found his tracks. He went that way. I think he is following something else because I don't see any more places where he was playing with the sand worms," Bálint stated.

"Is that the same way the clover tells us to go?" Zohar asked, pulling Goldie up beside Morah.

Morah nodded. "Yes, it glows that ways," she said.

"Can you make it glow toward some food? I'm so hungry," Jabir said with a sigh, climbing up onto Precious.

"I'm hungry, too," Alice said, rubbing her belly.

"So am I," Phoenix added.

Morah bit her lip. "I don't thinks it takes us to food." She looked at Zohar. "Can you finds us some food?" Morah asked.

Zohar sighed. He was hungry, too. Looking at the barren landscape ahead of them, he didn't see anywhere they might find food—unless they were willing to eat sand worms. He eyed the other children who were looking to him for guidance. He frowned when he realized that Leo was not the only one missing.

"Where's Spring and Hope?" he asked.

Phoenix grinned and pointed at the sand to their left. Zohar turned in his seat. The sounds of giggles ran through the group of children, momentarily distracting them from their hungry bellies. Less than ten feet from the group, Zohar could see the ground moving. A long line of sand worms was popping up into the air before landing with soft thumps back on the warm sand. They frantically began digging in an attempt to avoid being caught by the tiny, emerald green dragon who was following a wave of sand and trying to pounce on the poor worms.

Zohar turned to look at Alice. "She wanted to go with Spring," Alice replied with a grin.

He turned his attention to Morah when her stomach loudly growled. She gave him a sad look and rubbed her tummy again. Holding the clover close to her chest with her other hand, she released a long, mournful sigh.

"I wishes we had some yummy things to eat," she said.

Zohar's eyes widened when the four-leaf clover began to glow more intensely. Morah gasped and cried in delight when the clover began to rise in the air. He watched as it swirled above their heads and blinked in surprise when a large canopy suddenly materialized. Under the canopy's shade, a long table—laden with assorted food and drinks—appeared with benches on each side.

The roof of the canopy looked just like the clover—green with four heart-shaped leaves. The stem threaded through a hole in the table.

Zohar's mouth dropped open when he saw all the yummy food. He whipped his head from side to side as the other dragonlings rushed to the table.

"Spring! Hope! Food!" Phoenix cried out.

Hope's dragon rose up on her hind legs and sniffed the air. Her tail thumped against the sand several times. A second later, Spring's head poked up out of the sand. She sneezed before her eyes widened in delight upon seeing the canopy and what was beneath its shelter. Wiggling up out of the sand, she and Hope excitedly bounced past Zohar. Shaking his head in wonder, he slid off of Goldie and patted the symbiot.

"I think I'm going to like this adventure after all," he said with a grin.

Goldie sneezed and followed him to the canopy. None of the children noticed the small, golden sand worm watching them with delight. Shimmering in the sun, the sand worm dissolved into glittering specks of gold which rose up into the air.

Arilla soared across the sands. The symbiots would protect the children while she paid a visit to the Keeper of the Stories. After all, if wishes were to come true, even a Goddess needed a little help sometimes.

CHAPTER TEN

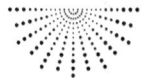

*C*alo gave Cree a lopsided grin and shrugged. If Cree could have reached his brother, he would have smacked him upside the head.

"This isn't funny," Cree growled.

Calo chuckled. "It is from where I'm standing," he replied.

Cree growled again and struggled to pull the lower half of his body out of the mushroom he had landed on and then began sinking into. The more he struggled, the more he sank into the soft fiber of the fungus. He really hoped that the mushrooms in this bizarre world weren't man-eaters.

"Will you help me get out of this?" Cree finally asked, resting his arms on the cap of the mushroom.

"Hold on," Calo replied, chuckling again at his brother's predicament.

"You know, you should be worried about our daughter," Cree reminded Calo. "She is all alone in a strange world and completely defenseless."

Cree watched the amusement on his brother's face fade. Calo gave him a brief nod before he shifted into his dragon. Cree followed his twin as he flew above the mushroom.

A flash of concern swept through him when Calo started to land next to him. He opened his mouth to warn his brother that he wasn't sure if the entire cap was soft, or just the small, bright blue spots on top which he had landed on. His unspoken question was answered the moment Calo landed and his feet began to sink into the soft exterior.

Calo lifted off again, hovering for a moment. Cree followed his brother's gaze and saw the long branch on the ground. Within seconds, Calo had swooped down, grabbed the long stick between his claws, and hovered above Cree with the stick extended toward him.

Wrapping both hands around the end, he nodded, and Calo pumped his powerful wings.

Relief flooded Cree when he began to emerge from the soft fungus. He looked down when his feet finally broke free. He grinned and looked up to let Calo know they were clear.

His eyes widened when he saw a pair of beady green eyes perched atop the stick staring at him. Startled, he released the end of the stick and fell. The sound of his dragon laughing was so loud inside his head that he barely heard his own grunt when he hit the ground and rolled.

He did hear Calo's muttered curse. Lying on his back, he saw the beady-eyed stick fall from his brother's grasp and raised his arms to protect his face. It didn't land. Cree peered through his arms and was surprised to see that a thin pair of wings had appeared along the slender branch. The stick-creature darted away from the brothers and was quickly lost within the forest of mushrooms.

Calo landed on the soft soil beside him and shifted back into his two-legged form. Slowly rising to his feet, he shot his brother a fierce glare of warning before he bent down to wipe off the white mushroom residue from his clothing.

"You should have seen...," Calo began before he clamped his mouth closed when he noticed Cree glowering at him.

"Not... a... word," Cree warned, pointing at his brother.

The amusement on Calo's face grew until his brother practically snorted from his struggles to keep it contained. Despite his best efforts, Cree's lips twitched. Shaking his head, he took a deep breath.

"Let's find the others before anything else unusual happens," he muttered, turning toward the trail.

~

"I don't like this world," Vox growled, turning in a circle. "It makes my hair stand up."

Kelan chuckled and dumped the water out of his boot. He looked over at Vox. The Sarafin King's hair was plastered to his head thanks to their jump into the wide stream to escape two Tasiers that were following them.

"You look like a drowned cat," Kelan commented, pulling his boot on before taking the other one off and emptying it too.

Kelan chuckled again when Vox bared his teeth at him. He distractedly listened as Vox muttered under his breath about how every time his family came to visit, there was some kind of catastrophe. First, it was Easter eggs, then it was almost getting eaten by ghost wolves in the haunted forest, then his hair caught on fire, and his son was almost blown up in a volcano, followed by booby-traps in a haunted house, getting knocked out while dressed as a giant rabbit, an unexpected trip to Earth through a portal, and now this!

Kelan was pretty impressed by how Vox was able to condense so many adventures into one long sentence without even taking a breath. He slid his boot back on and scooted over on the rock, so Vox could sit down.

Vox's nose wiggled as he pulled his boot off and looked inside. With a sigh, he stood up, walked over to the stream, and tilted his boot. Kelan couldn't hold back the bark of laughter when he saw a small fish fall out.

"I'd have eaten it if it had been worth the effort," Vox commented, sliding his boot back on before he removed the other and did the same thing.

"This reminds me of the story Trisha once told Jabir about a Puss-in-Boots, only you'd have the Fish-in-Boots," Kelan teased.

"Ha-ha," Vox sarcastically replied. "What now?"

"I think we should find the other men, find the kids, and then figure out where in the hell we are so we can get back home," Kelan said, standing up.

Kelan looked up when a shadow passed overhead. His dragon hissed out a warning, but it was too late. A pulse of red light surrounded him, lifting him up off his feet. He heard Vox utter a savage snarl and saw him shift into his leopard. Vox had only taken two steps before he was lifted off his feet as well. Immobilized, neither man could resist.

Kelan peered out over the large cavern as the beam holding him moved up. He was suspended between two bat-like creatures. On each creature were two warriors dressed in dark green and brown leather. Their skin was a pale green. Their eyes were a mixture of brown, green, and yellow. One warrior guided the bat-creatures while the other held a staff with a glowing red gem that reminded him of the ones they had used to defeat his uncle.

He was pretty sure his jaw would be hanging down if he could have moved it. The warriors were carrying Vox and Kelan toward the far end of the cavern where a large palace was carved into the rock face. Waterfalls flowed down into a valley lit with colorful mushrooms and glittering jewels. If he didn't know any better, he would think that he and Vox were about to find themselves in the mystical Kingdom of Glitter.

CHAPTER ELEVEN

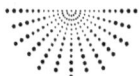

*S*andora: Kingdom of the Sand People

Tia hummed under her breath as she pulled a fresh scroll out of the cubby where she kept the finely woven sheets. She was diligently documenting the numerous stories of the Sand People. She knew it would take years to record and illustrate them all because there were so many.

Walking over to her workbench, she slid onto the seat and placed the scroll on the tilted drawing table that Jett had built for her. She frowned when she began to unroll the scroll and discovered that the sheet already contained writings and illustrations on it—and it wasn't in her handwriting, nor was it a tale familiar to her.

Reaching up, she secured the top of the scroll in place before sliding her hands down to do the same to the bottom. She scanned the beautiful illustrations. A soft gasp escaped her when the illustrations moved.

Fascinated, she began to read the story. It was the story of a group of fathers who had gone camping with their children. She continued reading, laughing when one of the little boys asked if he could eat the being called a Leprechaun. She moved her gaze to the illustrations as a broad-shouldered man moved his hands and spoke to his avid audience. His features reminded her of the woman who had brought life back to their world.

Tia drew in a shocked breath when she recognized one of the men sitting on a log near the fire. He was the man who had been with the Goddess Ariel. Enthralled by their story, she continued reading. Her lips twitched when she saw Tamblin's name as well as her own.

"Jett!" she murmured, staring at the image of her husband.

She touched the illustration with a combination of horror and fear. The love of her life had been thrown from his sand skimmer. Out of nowhere, a young creature suddenly appeared. At first, Tia thought the creature had crushed Jett, but as the image changed, she saw that he had cupped his paws around her husband and tossed away the sand worm that had attacked Jett.

Her heart ached when she saw the creature shift into a very young but very large boy. Tears glistened in his dark brown eyes. He sucked on his finger while looking down at Jett with wide accusing eyes filled with hurt. Her husband stood with his sword drawn.

"Oh, my love, you are such a meanie," she accused with a breathless, relieved laugh.

She continued reading until the story suddenly stopped. She frowned, unsure of what to make of it. Her eyes widened when she saw words suddenly appear as if the story were still being told. In these words, Jett was returning with the young creature following behind him.

A shout echoed through the open window of her office. Standing, she walked over to the window to see what all the excitement was about. Her lips parted in disbelief when she saw Jett and Santil appear through the entrance tunnel. Unfortunately, the black furred creature was too large to fit. The creature tried to wiggle his head through the passage, but the only thing that would fit was his short nose. He pulled back and sat down on the sand outside the entrance, his ears twitching as the guards yelled in alarm.

Concerned that the guards might hurt the child, Tia turned to exit the room. She glanced at the scroll and stopped in surprise when she saw the illustration showing her standing in front of the child. She quickly read the words unfolding before her eyes. Her lips parted in delight and a soft laugh escaped her. In the top left corner of the illustration, a golden figure lifted a finger to her lips and winked at her. Tia's eyes twinkled with merriment as she understood the adventure that was unfolding.

"I do believe the Goddesses are feeling mischievous," Tia laughed, before she quickly read more of the story. "It would also appear a visit to my brother is in order."

Deftly detaching the scroll, Tia rolled it up as she hurried out of her workroom. With the Goddesses guiding the adventure, she didn't think any harm would befall the young boy. Still, it was better to be safe than sorry.

"Are we's there yet?" Hope asked.

Phoenix wrapped her arm around Hope when the little girl yawned and leaned against her. After their lunch, Hope had crawled up onto Harvey with Phoenix, Spring, and Alice. Cree and Calo's symbiots trotted on each side of Harvey, who was now in the shape of a small, open transport that skimmed above the sand.

"I don't think it is much farther," Phoenix said, stroking Hope's hair back when a breeze blew it in her face.

"Here you go," Alice said with a smile, waving her fingers toward Hope.

Hope giggled when her dark brown curls suddenly twisted into rows of braids that wrapped around her head, complete with flowers.

Phoenix laughed in delight when Alice did the same to her hair. She reached up and touched one of the flowers in her hair.

"Looks! We's found Leo!" Morah suddenly cried out.

"Oh! I bet he's found something fun," Amber said, sliding off of Symba. "I'll race you, Jade!"

The four girls sat forward on Harvey to watch while Amber and Jade took off across the sand with the boys not far behind them. Phoenix giggled when she saw Leo trying to figure out how to get inside the large dome that shielded the city.

The small tiger cub had his nose pressed against the dome while his front paws were spread in an effort to keep his balance. He looked like he was trying to climb up on top of it, but he kept sliding off. Phoenix's lips parted when he suddenly hissed, his hair standing on end and he tumbled backward before lying flat on his belly.

"Leo!" Roam called, slipping and sliding down the sea of sand.

Leo looked up when he heard his name and shifted back into a boy. His black hair was standing up on end. He gave Roam and the others a toothy grin.

"Amber's, Jade's, you's gots to try this!" Leo said with delighted excitement in his eyes.

"What?" Amber said, reaching Leo first.

"They's gots zappers!" Leo reached out his left hand and touched the dome while at the same time he reached out his right hand to touch Amber.

Even from the top of the hill, Phoenix could see the thin thread of electricity jump from Leo to Amber. The sound of a snap in the air closely followed by Amber's loud squeal left Leo rolling in delight on the sand. A moment later, all the kids were shocking each other.

"Now I know why boys aren't so smart. They cook their brains," Spring observed, pursing her lips when she saw Roam with little wisps of smoke rising from his hair.

"Uh-oh, here comes Amber and Jade," Phoenix warned, her eyes widening when she saw the mischief in their eyes.

Alice grinned and raised her hands. Amber and Jade's dragons squealed when they felt the slight shock hit them. Giggling, they collided and rolled back down the hill into the boys.

"Oh, that was funny, Alice!" Spring said, clapping her hands.

"Funny, funny. Agains, Alice. Do it agains," Hope added, bouncing on Phoenix's lap.

Phoenix looked over at Morah. She frowned when she saw her cousin's bottom lip tremble. Nudging Alice, she nodded to Morah.

"What's wrong, Morah? I wouldn't hurt them," Alice said.

Morah shook her head and wiped at her face. "I's don't thinks this is where the Leprechauns lives. My dada can't fits through there," she said with a trembling lower lip.

"But, maybe whoever lives there might know where the Leprechauns live. Maybe this is where the Queen of the Wood Fairies lives," Spring said.

Morah shook her head. "I don't sees no woods," she replied with a doleful expression.

"Maybe... Oh, look!" Phoenix started to say before she stopped in surprise.

"Dollies! I wants dollies!" Hope squealed, reaching out her hands and wiggling her fingers.

Phoenix held Hope against her and shook her head. "I don't think those are dolls, Hope. They are moving on their own," she replied.

"I hope it isn't any of Amber or Jade's toys. They moves on their own all the time," Alice muttered.

The others quickly shifted from their tiger and dragon forms back into kids—well, all except for Leo as he had shifted back into his tiger form again. Phoenix slid Hope off of her lap and climbed down from Harvey. Reaching up, she helped the other little girl down. Alice and Spring followed behind her.

Phoenix watched Morah lift her head and ride forward on Crash. Her eyes glowed with delight when she saw the way the others parted to clear the way for her, even Zohar stood to the side. He caught her watching them and winked.

"Leo, no! You spits him out now!" Morah ordered, sliding off of her symbiot unicorn and pointing her Princess wand at him.

Leo opened his mouth and unrolled his tongue. A very agitated warrior pointed his finger at one of the other little men. He was huffing and puffing so much, that no words were coming out of his mouth. Leo looked up at Morah and shifted into a boy.

"Aw, Morah, I's wasn't really goings to eats him. I was justs playings," Leo said with a pained expression.

"Jett," a soft voice admonished.

One of the tall, slender warriors in the front turned when he heard the woman call his name in a chiding tone. He reached out and wrapped his arm around the shoulders of the warrior Leo had scooped up. The soggy warrior elbowed Jett in the stomach, and the sound of giggles rippled through the gathering crowd.

"I didn't tell the boy to do that—this time," Jett defended before he turned to his friend. "I'm sure he wouldn't have swallowed you, Santil," Jett reassured his friend.

Santil wiped at his damp shirt and glowered at Jett. "I will not be saving your ass the next time a sand worm knocks you off your sand skimmer," Santil replied in a calm voice.

"Yes, you will, because you know it would break Tia and our children's hearts to lose such a wonderful husband and father," Jett chuckled.

"You're Tia? Are you's the Keepers of the Stories?" Morah asked, sinking down onto the sand so she could look down at Tia.

Tia looked up, startled that Morah knew who she was. Tia nodded and smiled at Morah. Phoenix could see that the doll-sized woman held something in her hand.

"Yes, and you must be Morah," Tia replied.

Morah nodded. "Has you seen my dada? I's lost him," she sniffed before she started crying. "I's thinks the Leprechauns took him. Can you please helps us gets our daddies back?"

"I's gots two daddies," Hope added, pulling away from Phoenix so she could sit down in front of Tia. "They's really bigs and my momma and I's loves them."

"My daddy is really, really bigs," Jabir said. "My mommy says I shouldn't worry because I still have a lot of growing to do, so I can be likes him."

Phoenix held her breath when Spring grabbed her hand and pulled her forward. She could feel her sister's hand tremble, and she squeezed it. Spring drew in a deep breath and looked down at Tia.

"Phoenix and I miss our dad, too, but not as much as our mom would. She needs daddy," Spring said in a quiet voice.

"So do we," Phoenix added, smiling.

"I know," Tia said with a bow of her head. "I also believe I know where your fathers are. We must travel across the sands to the Kingdom of Glitter."

Everyone turned when Leo suddenly raised his hand in the air. Phoenix bit her lip when Morah turned and frowned at the boy. Lifting her chin, she pointed her Princess wand at him.

"What's do you wants, Leo?" Morah growled.

Leo gave her a pitiful look. "I'm starvings. Since I's not allowed to eats the little people, can I's please have somethings else?" he pleaded.

Phoenix touched Morah's arm. "I saved some sandwiches from our lunch," she said, pointing back toward Harvey.

"Thank the Goddess for the sandwiches," Santil interjected as they watched Leo's face light up with delight before he shifted into his tiger form and bounded away.

CHAPTER TWELVE

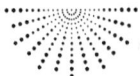

*P*aul warily kept his eyes on the two massive creatures gingerly walking beside them. He could feel the tension in the other men as well, yet the warriors surrounding them completely ignored the black-haired, red-eyed beasts that looked like a cross between a wild hog and a hyena. For the first time since this adventure had begun, even his dragon was wide awake and alert.

It's about time, he silently muttered to his other half.

I no like this world, his dragon growled, pacing back and forth.

"What's so funny?" Mandra asked under his breath.

His own dragon's anxiety matched the uneasy look on Mandra's face. These huge warriors weren't used to being on the other end of the food chain where things were bigger and deadlier than they were.

"My dragon isn't happy that his favorite snack tried to take a bite out of him or that these creatures look like they could swallow us without even chewing," Paul admitted.

"Mine isn't either," Trelon replied, glancing around at the beasts. "Something tells me that we wouldn't make it very far if we tried to escape."

"If we don't get eaten by one of those things, then we'd still have to fight off more than a hundred warriors and face the Tasiers. I'm sure I'm not the only one who noticed them feeding as we passed by," Mandra observed, a look of distaste crossing his face. "It is times like this when I wish Ariel or Jabir were here. Those two would have these creatures and the Tasiers eating out of the palms of their hands, regardless of how big they are. That would only leave us a few dozen warriors to contend with," he said with a rueful look.

"My biggest concern is the younglings. We don't know for sure if they are here, but what if they are and they encounter the creatures? Do you really think Jabir can control them?" Trelon asked.

"Like you said, we don't know for sure if they are here or still back in the forest. All I know is I need to find Leo. That boy is far too daring to be left this long unsupervised," Viper stated with a worried frown.

"Leo! Can you imagine the damage my two can do? I know they brought some of their newest contraptions. I'm still finding demented symbiots left over from Halloween in our apartments!" Trelon retorted with a strained chuckle. "My hope is if they are still in the woods, the symbiots would have guided them back to Mandra and Ariel's home. If they are here.... I don't want to think of all the trouble they could cause," he said with a sigh.

"Regardless of where they are, they have the symbiots with them. My Zohar is smart. He and the older younglings will help protect the younger ones," Zoran stated with confidence.

"Yes, but will the symbiots be as protective of Leo, Roam, and Alice?" Viper asked with a worried expression.

They grew quiet when the woman in front of them stopped and turned to face them. Her face was devoid of expression as she raised the staff and brought it down with a loud thud against the rocky surface of the ground.

A collective hiss escaped the men when vivid red threads of light streaked out in all directions. The two beady-eyed creatures on either side of them turned and disappeared into the shadows.

Paul blinked in astonishment when the mushrooms around him began to glow in a sweeping wave across the floor of the cavern. The lights changed colors, illuminating the interior section of the cavern until they could see a path leading into a brilliant glittering city. It was almost like a veil was swept aside. On the opposite end from where they were standing was a beautiful castle carved into the rock with waterfalls on its right side.

Despite the splendor surrounding them, it was the man striding toward them who captured their attention. Tall and slender like the others, his skin was a light green, and he had a regal confidence. The way all of the warriors came to attention could only mean one thing....

"The Leprechaun King!" Trelon hissed under his breath.

Paul drew in a shocked gasp. The man did look like one—well, if he thought of Leprechauns as tall and stately instead of short and somewhat rounded. The man's eyes narrowed, and Paul was confident he didn't miss anything in his scrutiny of them.

The King stopped in front of them. His gaze moved from one to the other before his lips pursed for a fraction of a second when another woman, who had the same green skin, facial features, and vivid red hair, hurried up behind him. The man took a deep breath before he spoke.

"I am King Tamblin... of the Leprechauns," he announced with an almost pained expression though his voice was cool and confident. "This is my sister, Tia."

"Hello," Tia said with a warm smile.

"What brings you to my kingdom?" Tamblin demanded.

Zoran stepped forward and introduced himself. "I am Zoran Reykill, King of the Valdier," he stated.

Ha'ven stepped next to Zoran on his left side. "I am Ha'ven Ha'darra, Crown Prince of the Curizans," he introduced himself.

Viper nodded to Tamblin. "I'm Viper d'Rojah, Prince of the Sarafin. I'm looking for a small black tiger cub with dark brown eyes. He likes to eat things that he shouldn't. Have you seen him?" he demanded.

Tamblin's eyes twinkled with amusement, but he didn't appear at all surprised by the introductions—or Viper's question. A frown creased Paul's brow.

Tia's eyes sparkled with excitement and merriment. She was biting her bottom lip in an effort not to laugh. Clearly, she was not the type capable of keeping a secret for long.

"King Tamblin, if I may explain," Paul said, stepping forward.

Tamblin turned to face him, a slight frown furrowing the man's brow. Tia leaned forward and whispered in Tamblin's ear, but Paul still heard her say his daughter's name, and he distinctly heard her say *'you know, the one with the princess gown and wand.'* Tamblin's lips twitched, and he nodded.

"You are the storyteller," Tamblin stated with a straight face.

Paul raised his eyebrows in surprise. "Yes," he replied.

A hint of a smile tugged at the corner of Tamblin's mouth for a moment—before he laughed outright. Paul looked around when many of Tamblin's warriors began to chuckle as well. He looked back at the King with a quizzical expression.

"It would appear that you and my sister have a lot in common. If you would follow me, I believe there is still more of the story to be told," Tamblin said with a bow of his head. The king raised his hand, and the warriors parted, stepping back and bowing in respect. Creon and Mandra each fell in step with Paul as he followed Tamblin.

"What did he mean by 'there is more to be told'?" Creon asked in a low, wary voice.

Paul chuckled. "Something tells me the kids are here," he replied under his breath.

"The kids?!" Mandra softly exclaimed, looking up and scanning the area.

"Do you think they were shrunk like we were?" Ha'ven asked, falling back to walk with them.

Paul shook his head. "I don't know. I never added shrinking to the story, so this is all new to me," he confessed.

Zoran gazed around them. "This is incredible," he said to Tamblin with a wave of his hand at the glittering city.

Tamblin smiled and glanced over his shoulder at them. "Thank you," he said.

"Tamblin, can you share what is going on?" Paul asked.

Tamblin nodded to his sister who was hurrying up ahead of them. "It would appear that a group of children are searching for their lost fathers and have decided that I, Tamblin, King of a magical species known as Leprechauns, must have spirited you away to the Kingdom of Glitter," he responded with a chuckle.

"Is that a yes, you've seen the cub then?" Viper asked with a growl of frustration. "My mate is going to skin me alive if I've lost him."

Tamblin laughed. "Yes, he is alive. I believe Santil is quite miffed with that one. He tried to eat him," he replied.

"Thank you, Goddesses!" Viper muttered in relief, lifting his hands and running them through his hair.

"Now all we need is to find Vox, Kelan, and the twin dragons," Ha'ven continued.

Tamblin raised an eyebrow. "We have found two more men. I fear we had to contain one. He would not cooperate," he said.

Ha'ven and Zoran grinned. "Vox," they both said at the same time.

Tamblin nodded. "I believe that is what the man named Kelan called him, along with a few other names," he stated, falling quiet as they walked through the city.

"Now, we just need to find the twin dragons," Trelon said.

CHAPTER THIRTEEN

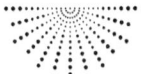

*H*ope's nose wiggled as a familiar scent floated in from outside. Sniffing, she tilted her head and stared at the open doors leading out onto the balcony. The older dragonlings were talking in hushed voices. Morah was asleep on the couch, and Leo was sitting on the table in his tiger form sampling food from each of the platters that were being brought in for them. Several of the women Tia had left with them were laughing as they watched Leo.

What's is it? she whispered to her dragon.

Daddies! I's smell daddies! her dragon replied with excitement.

Where? Hope asked, standing up from the floor where she was drawing.

Near. We find our daddies! her dragon insisted, pulling at her to shift.

Hope bit her lip and looked at the women. They were too busy watching Leo and his antics to notice that she was moving closer to the open doors. Focusing like her daddies had shown her, she slipped through the doors and onto the balcony.

She could feel her body changing. She embraced the feelings and gave herself over to her dragonling. A second later, the tiny emerald green dragonling was scurrying along the balcony.

Where is they? Hope asked.

Her dragonling paused and sniffed the air. She looked around until she saw movement on the cliffs near the waterfall. Her daddies were moving along the rocks toward a dark cave.

Daddies! Hope and her dragon squealed in delight at the same time.

The tiny emerald-green dragonling bounded across the balcony and leaped towards the railing. It took several tries to climb all the way on top of it. Shifting back into her two-legged form, Hope balanced on the railing and began frantically waving her arms.

"Daddies! I's here! Here's I am!" Hope called at the top of her voice. "Daddies! I's here!"

She saw both of her fathers turn their heads toward her at the same time. In her excitement, she took a step closer to the edge, clapping her hands when they saw her. Her lips parted to shout to them again when her foot slipped off the edge of the balcony railing. Unable to right herself, Hope twisted, her arms reaching out to her fathers and her eyes imploring them to help her as she fell.

"Daddies!" she screamed.

～

The cliffs near the waterfall:

A few moments ago

Cree looked over at his brother. They had made it to the far side of the cavern and had been scaling the rocky cliffs for the past hour. They had decided against shifting into their dragon forms after seeing the flying beasts with the warriors on their backs.

Their best bet was to stay in the shadows and work their way around to the palace. They were halfway there when Cree felt his dragon straining to break free.

What is it? he demanded, crouching on a narrow ledge.

"Do you sense something as well?" Calo asked, climbing up next to him and kneeling on one knee.

"My dragon is going crazy," Cree replied.

"Mine is too," Calo stated, looking down at the shimmering valley. "Look!"

Cree looked down. In the distance, he could see Zoran, Paul, and the others walking down a wide path. Two massive black beasts with glowing red eyes trotted on either side of them while a legion of warriors surrounded them.

"*Dragon's balls*! Where have we landed?" Cree cursed.

"It looks like we are the only two who haven't been captured. There are Vox and Kelan," Calo said, pointing to another section in the center of the plaza. "Looks like Vox isn't being very cooperative."

Cree turned to look at Vox and Kelan. Six warriors surrounded Vox who was pacing back and forth. From the flashing of teeth, it was obvious he was one very upset leopard. He curled his fingers around the edge of a rock when he felt his dragon hiss out a warning.

Hope! his dragon roared.

"Hope!" Cree said at the same time as his brother.

They frantically searched the valley below them until they heard a soft cry carried on the breeze. Cree's eyes widened in horror, and he rose to his feet. Calo stood up behind him, his hand raising and stretching out as if to stop what was about to happen.

"Goddess, no! Please, no!" Calo begged in a hoarse voice.

Cree's heart pounded, and he dove off the ledge at the same time as Hope slipped. Shifting, he didn't care about anything but reaching his daughter before she hit the ground. He reached out, calling to Calo's symbiot and his own.

The two symbiots appeared, diving over the balcony at an incredible speed. Even so, Cree could tell that they would all reach Hope a fraction of a second too late. There was no saving their beautiful, fragile, little girl from certain death.

CHAPTER FOURTEEN

*A*rosa watched the events unfolding with a heavy heart. This was all her and Arilla's fault. They had meddled with the natural universe. Aikaterina had always warned them that there would be consequences if they did. Still, she couldn't let the precious little girl die.

Focusing, she changed her shape and transformed into the corporeal form of the wood fairy that she had used before with the four-leaf clover. She reached out and wrapped her arms tightly around Hope, drawing the fragile little girl close to her chest before she slowly descended to the moss-covered floor of the cavern. The two symbiots landed on each side of her a split second later.

Arosa turned and spoke in a soft, soothing voice to the sobbing little girl and the two shimmering symbiots. The symbiots brushed up against her, trying to reassure themselves that their little charge was safe. She looked up as the twin dragons landed and shifted. The wretched fear on both men's faces tore through her, causing a rush of emotion that manifested into a physical pain inside her.

"Hope," Cree choked out, his arms reaching for his tiny sobbing daughter. "Daddy's here, my little dragonling."

"We're here. I'm so sorry, my little princess. We should never have left you," Calo said in a thick voice that trembled. "Goddess, how can we ever thank you for saving our daughter?"

"I'm not...," Arosa started to say.

"It's the Queen of the Wood Fairies!" a voice cried out behind them.

Arosa turned, her eyes widening when she saw the group gathering around her. Caught, she wasn't sure what she should do. She looked down when a tiny hand cupped hers.

"I's knew you was reals," Morah breathed, staring up at her with shining eyes.

"I... am?" Arosa said, wondering frantically where her sister was and what she should do now.

"King Tamblin, may I introduce the Queen of the Wood Fairies...," Tia began before she paused.

"Arosa.... My name is Arosa," Arosa replied, clasping her hands in front of her and folding her wings.

"Arosa," Tia said with a gentle smile. "Arosa, may I introduce King Tamblin, King of the Leprechauns of Glitter."

"I know.... I mean, he...," Arosa was at a loss for words.

She focused on her connection to her sister and was surprised when she couldn't feel it. Unsure of what to do next, she swallowed when Tamblin stepped forward and lifted one of her hands to his lips. She had never felt the touch of a man's lips. Startled, she pulled her hand away from him and curled her fingers in the fabric of her long gown.

"You are truly a gift to both my people and to our visitors. Thank you for your bravery in saving the child's life," Tamblin said, lifting his hand to tenderly brush a lock of hair back from her flushed cheek. "I have never seen eyes shimmer with gold the way yours do," he murmured.

"Does this means you's still wants lots of golds?" Morah asked with a frown, looking worriedly at the golden forms of Crash and Princess Buttercup.

Tamblin chuckled and shook his head. "No, my heart belongs to the people of Glitter. I invite you to join us in celebration of new friend-ships," he suddenly announced.

"That's goods because we's only gots two wishes left," Morah replied with a sigh, holding up the now rather tattered-looking four-leaf clover.

"Two? I thought we only used one," Zohar said with a frown.

"No's, I uses two. I's wants to meet the Leprechauns and for foods," Morah stated with a nod. "I's knows my numbers."

"Oh, I didn't think the first one worked," Roam replied, scratching his head before he looked around with a frown. "Does anyone know where Leo is?"

Arosa saw a flash of panic cross Roam's face. She was about to reassure him that the little boy was safe when a sound from the entrance to the palace drew their attention. She watched with a bemused expression as a man came running out.

The man was wearing a set of funny green clothes. One hand was holding his pants up while the other tried to grab the tall, black shiny hat that was about to fall off his head. On the right side of the hat was a large, four-leaf clover. Behind the man was a tiny, black tiger cub with a piece of green material hanging out of his mouth.

"I am not food!" the man yelled.

"Jett!" Tia chided, shaking her head and laughing as Santil ran by her.

"I swear I didn't do it, Tia. That tiger cub was waiting under the stairs," Jett said, watching as his friend finally tumbled into the foun-tain several yards away from them.

Arosa was delighted with the antics going on around her. Captivated, she—along with the other adults—watched Santil and Leo with amused expressions. The children, distracted by Santil and Leo, ran over to the fountain. Even little Hope wiggled out of her father's tight embrace and squealed with delight. Soon, the sounds of splashing water and children's laughter filled the air. Even Santil let down his guard, and with the help of Leo, who was in the shape of a little boy now, they began a water fight. The rest of the younglings quickly joined in.

"I guess we don't need Santil to dress up as the King of the Leprechauns anymore," Jett observed.

"No, though I have to say Santil made an excellent Leprechaun before the paint washed off of him," she said, wrapping her arm around her husband's and shaking her head.

"Well, it looks like we'll have a few green Leprechauns of our own before the night is over," Paul chuckled.

"I just hope it washes off or we are going to have some explaining to do when we get home," Zoran replied.

Arosa tilted her head and studied the playing children as a chain reaction of groans dominoed through the men as Zoran's words sank in. A soft chuckle escaped her. The children appeared to be unconcerned with their changing color.

With a sigh, she realized that she should leave. Arilla and she had already caused more than enough mischief. They would be lucky not to get a stiff reprimand from Aikaterina for this little adventure. Still, it would be worth a rebuke for the chance to spend a short amount of time with these species. They always filled her with their amazing essence of love, warmth, and curiosity.

"Let the festivities begin!" Tamblin announced to the people gathered around him. "Let us prepare a celebration for our new friends and a warm welcome to the Kingdom of Glitter!"

Cheers rose up. She started and took a step back. It was time for her to leave. Her hope of fading away soon dissolved when she felt a firm hand grasp her wrist. Tamblin turned to her, his eyes filled with determination.

"Not so fast, my beautiful Queen," he murmured. "Tonight, I would be honored if you would be my guest and sit by my side."

Arosa's head was nodding up and down even as an unfamiliar feeling beat in her chest. Lifting a slender hand, she rested it over her breasts. If she didn't know any better, it felt like... a heartbeat.

Sitting atop the fountain, Arilla chuckled at the stunned expression on her sister's face. Deciding she would have some fun as well, she waved her hand. Inside the massive cavern, millions of shimmering green clovers suddenly opened up under the mushrooms, lighting up the interior with a wondrous green glow.

CHAPTER FIFTEEN

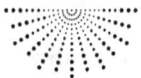

"I want to thank you for doing all of this," Paul said, standing beside Tamblin on the balcony later that evening.

"It was good for my people to have some excitement and to celebrate," Tamblin quietly replied.

"When Ariel told me about your kingdom, I never expected it to be like this," Paul admitted, gazing out over the vast, glittering cavern.

Tamblin smiled. "Lady Ariel gave us a gift we never expected nor believed was possible. She gave us the freedom to leave our home here, yet... I find I have no desire to live outside," he replied, remembering Lady Ariel's gift of the Tasiers.

Ariel had shared with Paul the story behind the people of Glitter. This moon was the birthplace of the Tasiers, the normally small, furry creatures that the dragons thought tasted like chocolate. Hunted to the point of extinction on their world, it had driven a divide between Tamblin's people centuries before. Some had taken shelter in the caverns, while others had learned to adapt to the harsh and very dangerous deserts that overtook their home.

It turned out that the Tasiers' waste was what gave the moon life—in the form of the fertilized mushrooms. When the last of the Tasiers were taken, the mushrooms and other plant life disappeared, leaving the small residents left behind vulnerable to the elements and predatory creatures such as the sand worms. Fortunately, the sand worms were the natural food source for the Tasiers.

"I almost forgot. I believe this belongs to you," Paul said.

He reached into his pocket and pulled out the gold coin he'd found on the ground earlier that morning. He studied it for a moment before he held it out to Tamblin. The other man took the coin, turning it over in his palm.

Paul saw Tamblin look down at the group sitting and chatting below. The man's eyes were on Arosa. His own eyes softened when he saw Morah sitting on her lap while Phoenix snuggled against her side.

"Who is she?" Tamblin asked with a frown.

Paul knew. His dragon had been very humble and deferential around her and the circle of symbiots near her stood out from up above. She looked up and caught his gaze. There was an expression in her eyes that he understood. He'd seen that same look in Trisha's eyes, Morian's too. Arosa was confused, hesitant, but also curious.

"She is the Queen of the Wood Fairies," Paul murmured, smiling at Arosa.

"Arosa," Tamblin murmured, his thumb stroking her image on the gold coin.

"It is getting late. Hopefully, we'll be returning home in the morning," Paul said, stepping away from the railing.

"It was an honor, Paul. If you or the other warriors ever return to our world, you will always be welcome," Tamblin said. He looked down at the coin in his hand before he held it out. "Please give this to your daughter as a gift. I hope it will help her to always remember her adventures in the Kingdom of Glitter," he said.

Paul raised an eyebrow in surprise. He reached out and took the gold coin. Nodding his head in agreement, he slipped the coin back into his pocket.

"Thank you again. Please give my thanks to Jett and your sister," Paul murmured. "Goodnight."

"I will. Goodnight, Paul," Tamblin said.

Paul turned and exited the balcony. He descended the curved stairs that led down to the garden where they had retired nearly two hours ago. Already, the symbiots were forming tents.

Paul nodded to the other men as they began gathering their children. His eyes followed the twin dragons as Cree cradled a sleeping Hope against his chest while Calo crawled inside their tent. Cree leaned forward and handed Hope to Calo. Paul could sense the love and fear still radiating from them.

He swallowed and closed his eyes. He knew what it felt like to think he had lost a daughter. Memories of Trisha's disappearance, the discovery of the sheriff who turned out to be a serial killer, and the knowledge that he might never see her again sent a remembered shaft of pain through him.

He opened his eyes when he felt the touch of a tiny hand in his. Looking down, he smiled at Morah's tired face. He bent down and scooped her up into his arms, tightly holding her against his chest.

"I have something for you," he murmured.

"What's?" Morah asked with a huge yawn.

Paul reached into his pocket and pulled out the gold coin that Tamblin had returned to him. Morah's eyes widened and she grinned. He watched as she wrapped her hand around the coin.

"Does this makes me a Leprechaun, Dada?" Morah asked, laying her head on his shoulder.

Paul brushed a kiss across his daughter's green forehead. He had a feeling it was going to take a few weeks before all of the green dye washed off. Until then, he and the other men would have some explaining to do to their mates.

"Yes, Princess, I guess it does," Paul answered, crawling into the tent Crash made.

He scooted over when Princess Buttercup climbed in beside Morah and curled up. Brushing her dark hair back, he pressed another kiss to her brow before lying down. Exhausted from the long day, he couldn't help but wish they would all wake up back home in the morning. He'd had enough camping for a while and wanted his mate.

She want you too, his dragon murmured with a sigh. *I keep watch.*

EPILOGUE

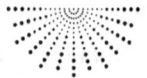

"*A*nd's Leo rans away and was playings with the sand worms. Oh, and he's tried to eats Santil. Santil wasn't really's a Leprechauns causes his skin wasn't really's green," Morah was explaining.

"Is that so," Morian said, trying to keep from laughing.

Morian watched her daughter pause and look up at her with a very serious expression. She bent forward and let the green water drain out of the bathtub. Another few baths and Morah might be back to her normal skin color.

"Is she still green?" Paul asked, leaning against the door jam.

Morian knew her eyes were full of laughter. She and the other women had been laughing non-stop for the past week, ever since the men and younglings had returned from their 'camping' trip. Ha'ven, Vox, and Viper had all scowled and swore to her that they would never go on another camping trip with her mate.

"Why ever not?" she and the other women had asked.

Of course, that was before they had seen the younglings. It had been hard to get a good look at the younglings when they were too busy chasing the new mob of emus that recently hatched. If they had, it might have made the outlandish story the men told more believable from the very beginning. It was only when the younglings elaborated on the men's versions that Morian realized that perhaps the story was not a tall-tale.

Morian reached for a towel and picked Morah up out of the tub. She turned and grinned. Paul shook his head in resignation and reached for Morah.

"I fear I'll never find my Princess again," he teased, rubbing his chin against Morah's damp hair.

Morah tilted her head back to look up at him. "I's can be a Princess Leprechaun. Alice mades me a new wand and Amber's and Jade's made it glows. I thinks they puts glowy worms in it," she explained, reaching for her new wand.

Morian didn't miss her mate's pained expression when he saw the wiggly bodies trapped inside the crystal tube. She would have to warn Trelon that the girls were having Spring dig up stuff again.

"I's wish we didn't has to use up all the wishes on my clover," Morah moaned for the hundredth time.

"Well, I'm glad you did," Morian stated firmly.

"Buts, mommy…. I wants a real unicorns and rabbits and…," Morah pouted.

Morian tapped her daughter on the nose. "And I needed Dada and you," she quietly said.

Morah wiggled her nose and giggled. "I's loves you, mommy," she said, lifting her arms.

Tears burned Morian's eyes as she wrapped her arms around Morah's towel-clad figure. She held Morah close for several seconds before she pulled back and sniffed.

"Okay, let's get you dressed and then bedtime," she ordered.

Within minutes, Morah was dressed in her Princess nightgown, curled up with her glowing wand of worms, and had both Crash and Princess Buttercup securely tucked in beside her. Morian bent over and kissed Morah's forehead before she stood back so Paul could do the same.

"Keep her safe," Paul quietly ordered the symbiots.

Turning out the light, Morian leaned against Paul as they walked to their bedroom. She turned the moment they entered and captured his lips in a passionate kiss. A shiver of need ran through her when he pressed her up against the wall next to the door. Reluctantly ending the kiss, she ran her hands up his chest and gazed up at him.

"What was that?" he asked in a voice still rough from their kiss.

Morian tilted her head and gave him a watery smile. "No more stories," she declared. "I couldn't bear to lose you or Morah."

Paul slid his arms around her and suddenly picked her up in his arms. Turning, he carried her over to their bed and laid her down. Brushing his nose along her neck, he whispered to his dragon to release the dragon fire.

"I've got the luck of the Irish in me, Morian, and a Leprechaun Princess with a magic four-leaf clover to prove it," he whispered. "We will always come home to you because everyone knows that home is where the heart is, and ours is right here with you."

Morian's lips parted in a gasp as Paul bit down onto the curve of her neck and released the dragon fire into her blood. For a moment, she could have sworn she saw the shadow of a four-leaf clover dance across the ceiling of their room before it disappeared in a blaze of rain-bow-colored fire.

To be continued…

Read on for the next adventure on the minor moon of Leviathan!

THE KING'S QUEST

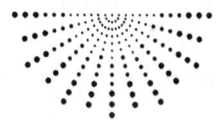

King Tamblin, ruler of the Kingdom of Glitter, prepares for battle after the aliens foretold by his sister, Tia, return to his world. He will stop at nothing to prevent the creatures from decimating their small moon again. Yet, there is little he or the Kingdom of the Sand People can do to stop the invasion. With all hope fading, Tia tells him that he must go on a quest to find the beautiful and mysterious Arosa, Queen of the Wood Fairies, and ask for her help.

Arosa, considered a Goddess on many worlds she visits, is stunned when a playful trick to entertain the Dragonlings of Valdier turns her life upside down. She never expects to feel the strange yet exhilarating emotions that Tamblin stirs inside her. Her kind were supposed to observe other species, not fall in love with them!

When the small bat she sent to guard over Tamblin alerts her that he is in danger, she will risk breaking the rules to protect him. Arosa recognizes love, but will the King return her feelings when he discovers that she is more than just the Queen of the Wood Fairies—that she has the power to not only save his world, but create entire galaxies?

PROLOGUE

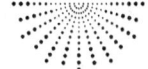

 ingdom of Glitter:

Minor Moon of Leviathan

Several Months Before the Present

"Oh, Arilla, what have we done?"

Arosa mentally sent the silent, dismayed question to her sister, Arilla, a moment before she solidified into the form of the Queen of the Wood Fairies. She caught the little girl who had slipped from the balcony high above and tightly cradled her. Hope, the daughter of the twin dragons, Cree and Calo, and their human mate, Melina, tearfully clung to her. She could feel Hope's heart pounding with fear. Mortified by the near tragedy, Arosa tenderly rocked the girl as she whispered soothing reassurances that she was safe.

Arosa landed outside of the palace where Hope had slipped from the balcony just seconds before. An instant later, Cree and Calo's symbiots touched down beside her. Their golden bodies were pressing against her to reassure themselves that their tiny charge was safe.

Arosa tried to smile reassuringly at the two almost identical dragons that swooped down, shifting into men a split second before they landed. The heart-wrenching fear on both men's faces tore through her, causing a rush of emotion that manifested into a physical pain inside her chest.

"Hope," Cree choked out, his arms reaching for his tiny sobbing daughter. "Daddy's here, my little dragonling."

"We're here. I'm so sorry, my little princess. We should never have left you," Calo said in a thick, trembling voice. "Goddess, how can we ever thank you for saving our daughter?"

Arosa stared at the two men. "I'm not...," she began before a child's excited voice pierced the air.

"It's the Queen of the Wood Fairies!" Morah Reykill happily exclaimed.

Arosa silently groaned when she saw the group of younglings gathering around her. Caught, she wasn't sure what she should do. When —not if—Aikaterina found out about this, Arosa suspected Arilla and she would be chastised.

She looked down when a tiny hand slipped into hers. Morah Reykill gave her a huge grin and an exaggerated wink, then stared at her with shining eyes full of excitement.

"I's knew you was reals," Morah cheerfully announced.

For a moment, Arosa struggled to remember who she was supposed to be. She frantically reached out to Arilla as she tried to decide the best way to handle the situation. Arilla's soft, lilting laughter filled her head when Tia, the Keeper of the Stories for the Kingdom of Glitter and their secret accomplice in this misadventure, stepped forward with a warm smile. Beside her was a stately man that inspired an unexpected response inside her.

Tia smiled and waved her hand between the man and Arosa. "King Tamblin, may I introduce the Queen of the Wood Fairies...," she began before she paused.

Arosa realized that Tia was waiting for her to introduce herself. "Arosa…. My name is Arosa," she replied, clasping her hands in front of her and folding her wings.

"Arosa," Tia repeated with a gentle smile. "Arosa, may I introduce Tamblin, King of the Leprechauns of Glitter."

Arilla! What am I to do? Arosa silently groaned to her sister.

Be the Queen of the Wood Fairies, sister, Arilla faintly replied.

An hour later, Tamblin smiled and distractedly nodded when one of the men sitting around the fire said something he didn't quite catch. Whatever it was must have been funny given the deep male laughter surrounding him. Tamblin was fascinated by the group of children as they joyfully played under the watchful eyes of their fathers.

He decided that tonight could only be described with one word—magical. It was hard to believe the strangers sitting around the fire were Valdier, Sarafin, and Curizan warriors. He remembered them being so much larger. It wasn't only the men sitting and chatting or the unusual children who shifted from one form to another who held his fascination, though. The beautiful enchantress sitting beside him was twisting his normal, stolid control into knots.

"Is everything alright?" Arosa asked.

Tamblin nodded. In an impulsive move, he reached down and cupped Arosa's hand. She stiffened with surprise and tilted her head, giving him a curious, shy look. He rose to his feet and looked down at her.

"Would you like to go for a walk?" he asked.

"I—yes, that would be nice," she answered.

Tamblin didn't miss the note of uncertainty in Arosa's voice. Paul Grove, one of the men sitting around the fire, looked up and gave him a nod. Tamblin bowed his head and smiled before guiding Arosa away from the group and along a cobblestone path. The stones lit up under his feet but not hers. It took him a moment to realize it was because she was floating beside him, not actually touching the cobblestones.

"Do you mind if I ask where your kingdom is? I have never heard of it before," he politely inquired.

Arosa gave him a startled glance and then quickly looked away. "It is in—the woods," she answered in a hesitant voice.

"Where though? The forests are just now growing back. How did you survive after the Tasiers were taken?" he asked, mentioning the small, furry rodents hunted almost to extinction by off-world traders.

"Not far. There is a forest that survived—to the west. That way," she said, with a wave of her hand, "on the other side of this mountain."

"That is north," he replied.

Arosa scowled at him. "Well, it is to the north," she said, floating a few steps ahead of him.

Tamblin tightened his grip on her hand and twirled her around. Arosa gasped when their bodies collided. He slowly lifted her hand to his lips and kissed her fingers.

"Tia has never mentioned Wood Fairies before," he said.

"King Tamblin," Arosa began.

"Please, call me Tamblin. As I said, Tia has never mentioned the Wood Fairies, but... I also have never asked about them," he continued.

Arosa nodded. "Then, that is why you haven't heard of me," she breathlessly replied.

"Queen Arosa, it would be an honor to show you my Kingdom, if you would permit me," he said, with a slight bow.

Arosa nodded again. Tamblin took a deep breath, released her hand, and held out his arm for her. She gave him an uncertain look before she threaded her arm through his.

A satisfied smiled curved his lips when she tightened her grasp on his arm. They continued along the path as it curved through a small mushroom forest to a gazebo by the river. When he needed a quiet place to sit and think, he often came here.

"How did you find your way to Glitter?" he inquired.

Arosa frowned. "I followed the men. They were looking for the King of the Leprechauns," she replied.

Tamblin's lips twitched at her tone. She sounded almost pleased with herself. He couldn't discern if she was telling him the truth or not. From the way she glanced at him, he suspected she was—but with a touch of exaggeration.

He chuckled and guided her up the steps into the gazebo. She released his arm and walked over to a small deck built over the water. He studied her face as she stared down at the colorful fish.

"Paul explained a little of what happened to them. It is a very interesting story." He paused when he heard the faint sound of music. "Would you like to dance?" he asked.

Arosa turned and faced him. Her wide eyes were filled with uncertainty. He walked over to her and held out his hand when she didn't reject his request. She hesitantly lifted her hand and placed her palm against his as he drew her other hand to his shoulder. He pulled her closer to him as they danced.

The magic of the night filled him with a sense of freedom he hadn't felt in years. Their steps were slow at first as she tried to follow his movements. He led, guiding her in the simple steps. They twirled, moving in a graceful circle. All around them, the bioluminescent spores rose into the air like floating candles while fish splashed in the water, trying to gobble up those that drifted too close to the surface.

The colors of the night danced across her lovely face, and Arosa appeared to glow. Her eyes shone with her joy, and her radiant beauty took his breath away.

He drew them to a stop when the music faded. His heart pounded in his chest as he released her hand and wrapped his arms around her waist. She looked at him with wide eyes and parted lips.

"I hope you don't think I'm too forward for what I'm about to do," he said in a low voice.

"What are you about to do?" she breathlessly asked.

Tamblin smiled and lowered his head. "This," he replied, capturing her parted lips with his.

Arosa stood frozen, unsure of what was happening or what to do when Tamblin kissed her. Well, she understood in theory what Tamblin was doing. She knew that to reproduce, species needed to interact physically.

She and her sister, Arilla, had lived among the dragons of Valdier and visited enough worlds to understand that the species developed affections for each other. In fact, she felt genuine affection for the dragonlings, the group of young children from the planet Valdier, and their friends from the worlds of Sarafin and Curizan. It was one reason she and Arilla enjoyed spending time with the children and their families, especially during their holiday celebrations.

It wasn't like they spent a lot of physical time with them. She and Arilla enjoyed observing the interactions between the adults and their offspring. There might have also been some curiosity about the physical relationship between the adults. It was impossible to be oblivious to that. She viewed it as research, for gaining a deeper understanding for the time when she and Arilla were permitted to create and seed their own worlds with life.

The twin sisters were still young compared to Aikaterina, Aminta, Xyrie, and the other remaining elders—not that there were many of them left. As Aikaterina's protégées, they were being tutored on how to observe the evolution of worlds.

Their species had been created at the same time as the universe. As the universe expanded, so had their travels. The Elders, the first of her kind, had learned how to harness the energy that had created them. She and Arilla first appeared on the outer fringes of the universe, when it was still young and expanding at an exponential rate.

Aikaterina had discovered them drifting, their life force fading into the icy darkness of space. She had given each of them part of her own essence. It was much the same way that the Valdier could support their symbiots—the living-gold creatures that the Elders nurtured.

Arosa leaned forward when Tamblin pulled back. She liked the feel of his lips against hers. There was an energy in their shared kiss that created a spark inside her. The breath from his soft chuckle brushed against her cheek.

"That was very... pleasant," she announced.

Tamblin laughed. "Yes, it was indeed very pleasant," he teased.

Arilla silently floated above her sister and the young King of Glitter. Arosa was positively glowing. The worry for her sister ebbed. Out of the two of them, Arosa was the most fragile. She suspected that Arosa's greater need for infusions of energy was why Aikaterina was so insistent that they should remain close to Valdier and the river of symbiots.

Aikaterina had already forbidden them from interfering again after their last attempt at *helping* had ended with them accidentally sending a human ahead in time. It had been impossible to remain just an observer when the young woman's selfless courage had saved her world. Aikaterina had warned them at the time, that when timelines crossed and were altered, it created different outcomes—with consequences sometimes not seen for centuries.

Arilla sighed as a sense of guilt washed through her. She wondered if being around the Valdier, Sarafin, Curizan, and their human mates was the reason she and Arosa were more inclined to push the boundaries of what they should and shouldn't do. Arilla bit her lip and decided she needed to check on their mentor.

She looked down again when Arosa's laughter swirled through the air. Her sister would be alright. Arosa could handle the situation here while she went back to check on Aikaterina.

After all, what could happen? The Dragonlings and younglings were reunited with their fathers and would soon be home. Arosa would then return to the hive, and the King—well, he would never know that the beautiful, gentle Queen of the Wood Fairies was actually a being far more powerful than any other creature he would ever meet.

Tonight will be a pleasant memory for both of them, Arilla thought with a pleased smile before she vanished, leaving her sister to enjoy her time as a fairy tale Queen.

CHAPTER ONE

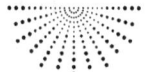

*K*ingdom of Glitter:

A Month Before the Present

"Tamblin, are you alright?" Tia asked, stepping out onto the palace balcony.

Tamblin nodded and glanced at his sister before returning his attention to the glittering kingdom in front of him. He wrapped his arm around her waist when she leaned against him. They stood in silence for several minutes, each lost in their own thoughts.

"It's beautiful. I think the festival this year is the best we've ever had," he said.

"They've always been wonderful, but I have to agree. I love this time of year when the mushrooms release their spores. You must come visit the Sand Kingdom again soon. The dunes are lit up at night. It reminds me of this place." She sighed with contentment. "Jett's mother and father are debating on whether they should change the name of their kingdom now that the desert is shrinking. The mushroom forests are spreading at a phenomenal rate. It reminds me of the old illustrations," she replied.

"It won't be for long if what you told me this afternoon comes to pass," he grimly replied.

Tia squeezed his arm. "My vision—maybe it won't come true," she wistfully countered.

He faced her. "Your visions have never been wrong, Tia. You know that. When the aliens return to our world, we must be ready this time. I want you to remember that there is plenty of room for expansion here. I will write a missive to Jett's parents, letting them know that the people of the Sand Kingdom are welcome here," he said.

Tia shook her head. "You know that would never work, Tamblin. Jett and his people will never give up their home without a fight," she replied.

He sighed. "If the aliens come, they may not have a choice. We are no match for their size and strength," he said.

Tia parted her lips as if she would protest, but she closed them and nodded instead. He pulled her into his arms and hugged her tight. Her slender figure had filled out again, and it felt good to hold her without fear of breaking her.

"How have you been feeling?" he asked.

She laughed and shook her head. "You ask me that every time you see me. I'm fine, Tamblin. My heart is beating normally. If it wasn't for running after my little Arielle, I would be the size of a Tasier with the way I eat," she retorted, referring to the furry rodents crucial to their small moon.

Tamblin chuckled and released her. "I think you are perfect." He turned and looked down over the kingdom again. "I can't believe how fast Arielle is growing. Though, I think she takes after your husband more than you," he said.

Tia put her hands on her hips, raised an eyebrow, and gave him a pouty look. "Why do you say that? I think she has a lot of my qualities," she replied.

He waved a hand over the railing. "You haven't been watching them, have you?" he asked with a laugh.

Tia followed the direction he was pointing. She uttered a very unladylike curse under her breath, hiked up her skirt, and left at a run. Tamblin laughed and shook his head. He gripped the railing and watched with amusement as Tia burst out of the palace below and hurried down the steps. His brother-in-law, Jett, was going to be in big trouble this time—not that he wasn't in it most of the time.

Jett appeared to have decided it was time to teach his petite daughter how to sword fight—albeit with a diminutive wooden sword. From the way Jett was yelping, hopping around, and rubbing at his shins, Tamblin was sure the man was already regretting the decision to give his little Arielle this lesson.

His niece also appeared to have inherited a bit of her personality from the woman she was named after. It had surprised him when Tia and Jett named their daughter after the alien female—but it was also fitting. Tia had foretold that a woman from a distant world would bring life back to the barren moon they called home. Once again, his sister had been right.

Lady Ariel of Valdier had discovered the Tasiers—gentle, furry beasts that ate the sandworms and fertilized their planet—at an off-world market. Unbeknownst to her, the creatures were essential to the ecological survival of the small moon and its inhabitants. The few she had brought with her had reproduced quickly—especially on a diet of sandworms. A chemical reaction between the spores buried deep in the sand and the excrement from the Tasiers caused forests of giant mushrooms to grow. The mushrooms rose from the vast deserts, cooling their world and bringing the much-needed cleaner air and rain.

Tamblin chuckled when he watched Jett laughingly trying to evade the dual attack of Tia and little Arielle. The sounds of boots against the polished stone floor pulled him away from his view of the activities below. He frowned when he saw the brooding expression on his General's face.

"What is it?" he demanded.

General Brant and two of his men halted at attention. Brant bowed his head in greeting before meeting his gaze. "King Tamblin, it is as you warned us this morning. We have spotted alien ships to the north," Brant responded.

Tamblin clenched his fist. "How many?" he demanded in a hard voice.

"Two, your Grace," Brant answered.

Two—so far. This would be just the beginning if history were to repeat itself. While Mandra Reykill, a Dragon Prince of Valdier, had declared the moon a sanctuary, the price for Tasiers was too tempting for some traders to resist. The dragon-shifters had long considered the small rodents a delicacy.

Now that the mushroom forest was thriving, the gentle creatures flourished. The moon was finally healing from the predation. Now it was being threatened again.

Tamblin gave a brief nod. "I want you to gather an elite reconnaissance team. See if you can board the ships without being detected. We need to know how the ships operate and discover if there is a way to disable them," he instructed.

Brant frowned. "If we disable the ships, it will trap the aliens on the moon," he warned.

Tamblin gave him a grim smile. "Yes. It is vital we have a strategy that will level out the battlefield. We are no match for their technology or their size. We will need to use what we have to our advantage. For now, we should assess the situation and gather as much information as we can," he replied.

"I'll gather a team, and we'll leave this evening," Brant said with a bow. Turning on his heel, he left.

Tamblin looked out across his kingdom again. The sounds of music and laughter resonated throughout the cavern. Illuminated mushrooms growing in thick clusters with brilliant colors released spores that looked like floating candles. Soft breezes that blew through the open vents would help carry most of the seeds outside where they would mix with the other spores.

The mood of his people had changed over the past few years. The restored balance of the moon brought feelings of joy and hope, while the discovery of other clans outside of the cavern brought a chance of survival. Tia's union with Jett had paved the way for increased trade and introduced the possibilities for new relationships among the clans.

He briefly closed his eyes when a shaft of yearning pierced him. The memory of Arosa, Queen of the Wood Fairies, flashed through his mind. He had not seen her since the night the men and children of Valdier had visited. His responsibilities always seemed to impede his own desires.

There hadn't been a day since then that he hadn't thought about Arosa. He would remember that magical night with her for the rest of his life. Memories burned inside him: the way her four small transparent wings hung down her back like a cloak, the way her long hair, its vibrant color like flames capped by a crown of tiny white flowers with dark red berries, fell over her shoulder, and the rosy hue of her lips after he kissed her. He would never forget how her brilliant green gown fell in layers around her, a striking contrast against her red hair and silky skin. Her intellect and wit had truly captured his admiration.

"Tamblin."

He turned when he heard Jett call his name. Lost in thought, he had missed the sound of Jett's approach. He forced a smile of greeting on his lips.

"Jett. I see you escaped your wife and daughter relatively unscathed. It looks like you might have a bruise under your eye by tomorrow," he mused.

Jett touched the tender spot under his left eye. "Arielle caught me with her sword while doing a backhand twirl. She said she is a dancing warrior princess," he chuckled before growing somber. "Santil found me. He said the scouts had spotted two alien transports."

"Yes. I've sent a team to do reconnaissance," he said.

Jett nodded. "I've done the same," he replied, walking over to the railing.

"I was going to send a missive to your parents. I want you to know that the Sand People are welcome here," he said.

"I appreciate the offer and will convey your message to my parents," Jett replied.

Tamblin didn't miss the way Jett's hands tightened on the railing, nor the way his lips pursed. They stood in silence, looking out over the festivities. He was about to say something when Jett spoke.

"Perhaps they will leave. The Dragon Lords promised to protect our moon. Surely whoever the traders are would not dare cross such powerful creatures," Jett growled with frustration.

"Greed can be more powerful than the need to survive, Jett. Generations ago, our ancestors saw what it could do. Almost three-quarters of our people died because of hunger, loss of habitat, or through the aliens' careless harvesting of the Tasiers. Only a few clans survived the devastation by the aliens, and we didn't even know about each other until recently," Tamblin reminded him.

"We can't let it happen again, Tamblin," Jett passionately declared.

"It won't. We will fight them," he replied, his eyes glued on Tia and little Arielle's laughing faces.

"Is there any way to get in touch with the Valdier?" Jett asked.

"They will know. The question is if they will discover it in time," he reluctantly admitted.

Jett frowned and faced him. "What do you mean?" he asked.

Tamblin sighed. "The Valdier promised to protect our planet. The last time Lord Mandra returned, he asked me if I would agree to the Valdier sending a scientific research ship here to install devices that would monitor the rehabilitation of the moon. I agreed, and now once every new moon, the information automatically transmits to them through these devices," he said.

"My parents mentioned it to me when you relayed the message to them, but where did they install them? I haven't seen any of the devices," he replied with a frown.

"There are four within a hundred-mile radius. One in each direction. I was told that if there is a dramatic change in the readings, it will trigger an alert, and someone from Valdier will come," Tamblin explained.

"It will be another thirty days before the moon circles the planet. Our historical scripts state that it took less than half that time for the population of the Tasiers to drop to critical," Jett growled with frustration.

"There were more ships," Tamblin pointed out.

Jett shook his head. "There were a lot more Tasiers, too," he countered.

Tamblin nodded. "Let us hope that these two ships are the only ones and we can discourage them from staying," he said.

"How do you propose to do that?" Jett muttered.

Tamblin sighed. "By any means necessary. We'll start with the Guardians," he said.

Jett shuddered. "Are you sure? Those beasts are as dangerous as the aliens," he muttered.

"That is what I am hoping," Tamblin grimly replied.

CHAPTER TWO

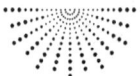

*M*inor Moon of Leviathan:

Present

Tamblin stared out at the lights flickering across the vast mushroom-covered plains. His heart ached when he heard the frightened squeaks of the Tasiers and the sharp snap of a trap. Despair filled him when he saw the poachers trying to reach the traps before his or Jett's men could.

The last weeks had grown decidedly more perilous. The two transports had become four, then six, and eight. He had ordered General Brant and his elite squad to disable the transports, but the aliens repaired them almost as quickly as they sabotaged them. It had finally become too dangerous. The poachers had set traps, injuring two of his warriors. Another six men had been trapped inside a transport that was about to leave the planet and they had barely made it out.

Tamblin released a sigh when a furry head nudged him. Oversized brown eyes with gold flecks in them gazed back at him with a solemn, inquisitive expression. He lifted his hand and gently scratched the adolescent bat behind one of its oversized ears.

"It's alright, Batty. Let's hope Jett and his teams get to the traps before the poachers," he tiredly said.

Exhaustion fogged his mind. This was the third week that he, Jett, and a combined force of soldiers from Sandora and Glitter were out all night. The poachers had begun patrolling when they realized that their traps were being sabotaged.

Batty nudged him again and turned his ears in the direction of the bouncing lights. Tamblin nodded his head in acknowledgement. Batty wanted to fly, and Tamblin needed something to lift his spirits.

"Your mistress would be very proud of you," he affectionately said.

Batty wiggled his ears back and forth, making Tamblin laugh. He stroked the bat for another moment before he turned and climbed onto the saddle strapped between its wings. He reached up and adjusted the night vision goggles over his eyes. With his focus on the vast plains below, he gripped the reins and tapped his heels to Batty's side.

"Let's have a little fun," he said.

Batty twitched his ears back and forth with delight, then jumped off the edge. Tamblin leaned forward and tightened his thighs against the saddle as they soared downward until finally, Batty began flapping his wings.

The wind brushed against his face as they flew through the night. It was going to be another long one. From the air, he followed Jett's team as they moved quickly to release the Tasiers that had unwittingly entered the traps.

"To the left, Batty," Tamblin instructed, leaning in the saddle.

The bat darted in front of one massive poacher. The man stumbled back several steps and swiped an enormous hand in their direction. Batty twisted in midair, changing directions. The man tried to follow their movements, twisting around so fast that he lost his balance.

"Damn creatures," the man growled with frustration.

Tamblin gritted his teeth when the man pulled a laser pistol from his waist and aimed the weapon at them. He leaned forward and Batty swerved. Tamblin winced when the super-heated blast from the laser narrowly missed them.

"*Dragon's balls, Macron!* Are you trying to kill me?" another poacher yelled when the blast sent him diving for cover.

"Sorry, Harron. These bats are driving me crazy," Macron shouted back, quickly holstering his weapon.

"You shoot that thing again and it will be more than the bats you'll have to worry about. The trap is empty again. I swear when I find out who is releasing the furballs, I'm going to roast them," Harron said.

"This one is empty too. I hope the others are having better luck than we are," Macron replied, kneeling next to the trap.

Tamblin saw Jett and Santil crouching behind a large mushroom only a few feet from Macron, which was too close for comfort. They couldn't keep this up. It was only a matter of time before someone was killed.

The sound of another trap springing and the squeal of a Tasier pulled him away. Batty flew in that direction, trying to reach the poor creature before the two poachers. Tamblin tensed, preparing to jump.

This will be another close encounter, he grimly thought as he released his grip on the reins and fell toward the large mushroom that would soften his fall.

～

Valdier:

The Hive

Arosa lay along the bank of the river of symbiots and moodily swirled a finger in the flow of gold. Warmth flowed upward through her outstretched arm. She sighed when some of the gold formed into fish and jumped. The scene reminded her of the magical night several months ago.

An uncharacteristic feeling of frustration flashed through her, and she sat up. She growled when the symbiots formed an image of Tamblin. They were reacting to her thoughts—and her longings that were growing stronger every day.

"This should not be happening," she snapped.

The symbiot gold Tamblin melted back into the river. Arosa stood up. She was alone at the moment—thankfully. With a sigh of resignation, she reached out to her sister.

Arilla, I need your guidance, she confessed.

Silence greeted her, the same silence that had surrounded her since her return from Glitter. She floated over to a boulder. Time normally meant very little to her species, but the last few months had seemed endless.

Her mind had replayed the magical night over and over. She felt guilty for her desire to go back in time to relive it, but a smile played on her lips as she closed her eyes and floated higher in the air. The wind became music in her ears.

She lifted her arms and twirled, dancing the way she had with Tamblin. She had repeated the movements so many times, she could now gracefully dance. A wave of symbiots rose from the river and formed Tamblin again. They had been her dance partner, but even their warmth could not replicate the feeling of being in his arms.

As the music faded, she opened her eyes. She traced the curve of her symbiot partner's cheek. The gold shimmered under her fingertips as it recognized her loneliness and longing.

"What is wrong with me?" she asked in a confused voice. "There is a beating in my chest that I don't understand, and I yearn for his touch. What is it that causes me to want to be with him? To hear his voice, his laughter, and to touch his lips with mine?"

She touched her mouth as she remembered his kiss. The symbiot Tamblin shifted into a bat. She shook her head and scowled at it.

"I know," she grudgingly said, turning away.

It would be so easy to spy on Tamblin. In fact, she had done so the first few days after that night, but guilt and other unfamiliar emotions plagued her, so she had forced herself to stop. At least she knew he was safe.

She floated over to a pillar and studied the star chart engraved on it, locating Tamblin's small moon. She looked at the platform and then down at the main gateway. Aikaterina and her sister still had not returned. There was no telling when they would. If she opened the main gateway, others of her kind would immediately sense it.

She looked at the pillar again. If she opened a very narrow gateway to the past, she could relive the night one last time. Perhaps the night was not as wonderful as she remembered.

"Just once, then I will never relive it again," she whispered.

The symbols on the pillar glowed as she sent the mental command. A hologram of the glowing star chart appeared before her. She touched the galaxy, pulling the moon into view. With a twirl of her fingers, time reversed until she saw the images of dragonlings. She replayed the night, following the events as they unfolded.

Her heart ached when she saw Hope's excitement turn to terror, the moment Morah gripped her hand so that she couldn't escape, and when Tamblin cupped her hand and helped her to her feet.

She stared up at the platform. The time when she was standing in Tamblin's arms appeared on the platform. She floated until she was level with the ghostly vision of her past.

"Just this one time," she promised herself and floated forward, merging her present self with her past.

A soft gasp slipped from her. Tamblin caught the sound when he kissed her. Arosa melted in his arms, wishing she could keep this moment frozen for eternity.

The Kingdom of Glitter:

Several Months Ago

"That was very… pleasant," she announced.

Tamblin laughed. "Yes, it was indeed very pleasant," he teased.

Arosa leaned forward and parted her lips when Tamblin kissed her again. She wrapped her arms around his neck and threaded her fingers through his hair. She could sense his surprise—and feel his growing desire. She sighed in regret when he reluctantly pulled back and gazed down at her.

"Arosa—I…."

She laid her fingers against his lips. "I want you to know that tonight is a night I will never forget, Tamblin," she confessed.

He frowned, slightly shook his head, and captured her hand in his. "You say that as if we will never see each other again," he said.

"My… kingdom differs from yours," she replied, pulling out of his arms.

He tightened his grip on her hand. "Things are different now. With the Tasiers' return, the mushroom forests are thriving again, and the threats have been mitigated. There is no reason we can't continue to see each other," he protested.

A pang of guilt pierced Arosa. How did she explain to Tamblin that she was not who she was pretending to be? As far as she knew, there had never been one of her kind who fell in love or stayed with another species. It was not their way.

She pulled away from him, fluttering her hand to her chest as she realized what she had just thought. Shock and confusion swept through her. Was it possible that she—a being made of pure energy—could experience love?

"Arosa, perhaps I've overstepped my boundaries, but I have to confess that I've never felt this way about anyone before. I want to see where it leads. A union between our two kingdoms could only strengthen them," he said,

"A union—?" she repeated, looking up at him in shock.

Tamblin groaned and shook his head. He reached out and cupped both of her hands in his. It was impossible for her to look away.

"That was very forward of me... but, please, hear me out. I know that we've just met, but I believe that there is a connection between us too powerful to ignore. This is an extraordinary night and I... I would like to explore where it could take us. What I'm trying to say is... I want to get to know you," he declared.

"Tonight...," she began, pausing and reaching out to her sister in desperation as she tried to think of what to say.

"We'll start with tonight," he agreed with a tender smile, misunderstanding her hesitation.

She nodded. Even though Arosa knew what was going to happen, she embraced the evening. Reliving the night over again was as magical as it had been the first time—though it seemed shorter.

All too soon, they were returning to the palace. She kissed each dragonling's forehead when they came up to wish her a goodnight. An unexpected burning stung her eyes when Morah tugged on her skirt. She knelt, looking the little girl in the eyes.

Morah touched her cheek with tiny fingers. "I wants you to knows that if you ever needs help, I will helps you. I'm goings to be a Priestess one days," she said.

Arosa smiled. "You will be a very good Priestess to the symbiots, Morah," she replied.

Morah nodded. "I's knows a lots 'causes I'm smart likes my mommy and daddy." Morah threw her little arms around Arosa's neck. The goddess blinked in surprise. "Thanks you for making my wishes come true. For my last wishes, I'd like for all the daddies and us to be bigs again so we can goes back home to our mommies."

"When you wake, your wish will have come true," Arosa promised.

"I hopes your wishes comes true too," Morah whispered in her ear before giving her a kiss on her cheek and stepping back.

Arosa stood and watched as the little girl, her skin dyed green from playing in the fountain and princess gown stained with dirt from adventuring through the land, ran over to her father. Deep in her heart, Arosa knew it was time for her to leave, but she didn't want to. She stared wistfully at Tamblin. He was talking to Paul, but she could feel his focus on her.

Anguish filled her as she relived the last few hours that she would ever have with Tamblin. A part of her wanted to pull away so she wouldn't have to say goodbye to him again, but another part wanted to savor the beautiful memory that came next.

"I've had a room prepared for you," he said.

She nodded, gripping his hand. They walked in silence up the steps into the palace. She followed him up the stairs to a long corridor on the third level. He slowed as they neared a set of double doors.

"I hope you will be comfortable. My room is next door should you need anything," he said as he turned and faced her.

"What if I need you... to stay with me tonight?" she quietly asked.

CHAPTER THREE

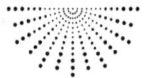

*M*inor Moon of Leviathan:
Present Day

"Tamblin, call them back," Jett shouted.

Tamblin lifted the curved horn to his lips and blew. The Guardians skidded to a stop. They were boar-like creatures with long tusks, sharp quills, and red eyes that could see in pitch darkness. One beast snarled when a blast from a poacher's laser pistol grazed it.

They couldn't afford to lose any more of the creatures that protected them. The poachers had already killed five of the beasts. Tamblin pulled back on his reins, directing Batty to follow the retreating warriors.

They were losing the war. Hundreds of Tasiers were being loaded onto the ships by the hour. Tamblin and his allies could no longer keep up with the traps. The poachers had modified the locking mechanisms, making the cages virtually impossible for his and Jett's forces to open them and free the trapped Tasiers.

They also had a bigger issue. One alien now knew about their existence and the man was hunting them. It was only a matter of time before the other poachers believed him.

Batty flew to a tall outcropping of rocks a short distance away. Nature and the weather had sculpted the various layers of rocks until it looked like slabs had been stacked on top of each other. Batty turned and gripped a large slab by his feet under a low overhang of rock.

Tamblin released his grip on the saddle, and slid off, landing on the ledge below. He lifted the horn to his lips again. He gave two long and one short blast. The Guardians responded by melting away into the night, disappearing down camouflaged holes that would lead them back to their caves.

He lowered the horn to his side when Jett's skimmer swung around an outcropping of rocks and came to a stop nearby. Jett dismounted and climbed toward his position. Tamblin reached down, gripped Jett's hand, and pulled him onto the ledge. Jett shook his head and gazed out at the trampled fields of mushrooms.

"They outnumber us, Tamblin. Even with our combined forces, we are no match for the aliens," Jett said.

"You're bleeding," he replied.

Jett grimaced and touched the wound on his temple. Tamblin walked over to Batty and pulled out a small first aid kit from his saddlebag. He motioned for Jett to sit on a rock.

"What are we going to do? We need help, Tamblin. At the rate they are harvesting the Tasiers, there will be none left by the end of the month," Jett commented.

Tamblin looked up when he saw a fire flare up. The poachers were using long wands attached to tanks to burn the mushrooms. Their newest tactic helped to herd the Tasiers in the direction they wanted and forced his people into retreat since they had no place to hide.

"How far are they from Sandora?" Tamblin asked.

Jett winced when Tamblin pressed a cloth coated with a disinfectant against the cut on his forehead. "A week if they stay on their current course. If any more come or they spread out, it would take less time. Father and Mother have instructed the citizens of Sandora to move to the underground chambers," he confessed.

Tamblin frowned and shook his head. "Even that isn't safe, Jett. You heard them. Now that an alien is aware of our existence, he has set traps to capture us. Once he or one of the others finds the city, it will confirm what he has been telling them. Sandora will be destroyed," he said.

Jett nodded. "They will think of us as freaks and oddities to be sold and put on display for credits. I remember their joking comments," he bitterly stated.

He finished bandaging Jett's wound and packed the remains back into the kit. Jett murmured his thanks and stood. Tamblin could see the weariness in Jett's eyes. A sense of hopelessness threatened to overwhelm him when he saw the flames rising into the night sky and the thick plumes of smoke.

"We need help," he said.

"All we can do is hope that the sensors the Valdier placed have triggered an alert and they will come in time," Jett tiredly replied.

Tamblin pursed his lips. Even if the sensors were triggered, by the time the Valdier arrived, nothing would remain—including themselves.

"Jett, you need to convince your parents to evacuate Sandora to Glitter. We have the shields, the Guardians, and the protection of being buried deep within the mountain. Sandora is too vulnerable," he said in a hard voice.

There was no more time to debate the decision. Tamblin's brother-in-law stared out into the burning night with haunted eyes. There was no trace of the fun-loving man he used to know.

"I will tell them," Jett promised.

Three days later, Tamblin stood on the balcony watching as the last caravan of refugees from Sandora entered the cavern. The mood had been somber but filled with determination.

Construction crews from Glitter and Sandora continued to work around the clock, widening new sections of the cavern for the new arrivals. Merchants and farmers focused on giving each family supplies.

Roan, Jett's father and the King of Sandora, and Ladora, Jett's mother, guided their people to the finished levels. A movement from above caught Tamblin's attention, and he watched Batty release his grip from where he was hanging and fly down to the balcony, landing on the narrow railing. He chuckled when Batty lifted his chin and wiggled his nose.

"I don't think I've ever seen a bat this affectionate, especially after being around you for so long," Tia teased, walking up and standing beside him.

He started with surprise and lifted an eyebrow. "I didn't hear you come in," he said, frowning when he saw that she was alone. "Where are Jett and Arielle?"

Tia scratched Batty behind the ear. "Jett is helping his parents and Arielle is playing with some new friends. I needed to speak with you alone," she said.

"What's wrong?" he asked.

"I've had another vision," she confessed.

Tamblin's stomach clenched with worry. Batty nudged his hand, and he realized that he had threaded his fingers through the fine hair along Batty's neck. He forced his fingers to relax.

"What did you see?" he warily inquired.

She looked away from him to Batty. "You must go on a journey," she replied.

He stared at her with a confused expression. "A journey? Now? When our kingdoms… our very existence is in jeopardy?" he asked in a voice laced with skepticism.

Tia nodded and looked at him again. "Yes. It is the only way to save our world and our people," she answered.

"Tia." He shook his head. "Where am I supposed to go?" he asked.

She paused her stroking of Batty, and was silent for a moment.

"You have to find the Queen of the Wood Fairies," she finally said.

"Arosa? You are saying I have to find Arosa?" he repeated incredulously.

Tia turned emotion-filled eyes to him. He could see the truth of her conviction in them, but there was also something else. She looked —pensive.

"What aren't you telling me?" he quietly asked.

She reached for him. He gripped her hand, gently squeezing it in reassurance and studied her face. Tears glistened in her eyes. He pulled her into his arms and hugged her.

"I don't want you to get hurt, Tamblin," she whispered.

He pulled back and studied her face again. "Tell me what you saw," he instructed.

"Arosa has the power to save our world," she said in a slow, measured tone.

"But—" he added.

"But—she also has the power to hurt you," she replied.

He shook his head in denial. "Arosa would never hurt me. If she has the power to save our world, then I will find her and bring her back," he said in a confident voice.

"I know this is what must happen, but Tamblin—please be careful," Tia said.

Tamblin kissed her forehead, released her and stepped back. "I will. I'll find her, Tia," he reassured.

He motioned to Batty. The small mammal released his grip on the rail and launched into the air. Tamblin jumped up onto the railing and hopped onto the back of the hovering bat. He slid his feet into the stirrups, unwound the reins from the horn of the saddle, and looked at Tia. She stared back at him as if she wanted to say something more, but she raised her hand instead.

"I'll return as soon as possible," he promised, tapping Batty's sides.

"Be sure that you do!" she cried out behind him.

CHAPTER FOUR

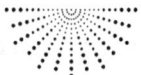

 aldier:

Paul Grove looked up from the tablet he was reading when his wife, Morian, came out of the kitchen. There was a worried expression on her face. He placed the tablet aside.

"What's wrong?" he asked.

She looked at him with a crooked smile. "Have you noticed anything unusual this evening?" she inquired.

He frowned and looked around the living room. The coffee table had a variety of toys covering it. Crash, their symbiot, was sprawled out on the balcony. The aroma of cooking food made his stomach growl. Everything appeared normal. In fact, it was downright peaceful.

His eyes widened. "Morah," he muttered.

She chuckled and nodded. "I haven't seen her in almost an hour. By now she's usually at the table moaning about how she is starving and we never feed her," she replied.

"I better check on her," he laughed as he got up from his chair.

"Tell her dinner will be in ten minutes," she called after him.

He scooped up several of his daughter's dolls as he walked down the hallway. Turning the toys in his hands, he shook his head. His oldest daughter, Trisha, had played with soldiers—real life ones. They were polar opposites about some things.

"But the same in others," he chuckled, looking at the princess doll in the flowing gown wearing a laser pistol at her hip.

He paused outside of his daughter's door and frowned when he saw it was closed. Morah never closed her door. He reached out and gripped the doorknob. The door was locked.

Surprised, he listened. He could hear her talking. He gently knocked on the door.

"Morah, honey, unlock the door," he said.

"I busy, Daddy," Morah called through the closed door.

Paul frowned and looked at the door with a raised eyebrow. "Busy?" he repeated to himself.

He knocked on the door again. "Morah, can you open the door, please. Mommy said dinner is almost ready. You need to get cleaned up," he replied.

"I can't eats right now. I'm busy," Morah responded.

He studied the door and wondered what was going on. Morah was talking again but obviously not to him. Curious, he pressed his ear to the door.

"You in loves. I know becauses my mommy and daddy has that weirds look in their eyes too when they talk about each others," Morah was saying.

Paul pulled back and gripped the doorknob again. "Morah, who is in there with you?" he demanded.

He stepped back when the door knob rattled. His eyes widened when his petite daughter scowled up at him with a disapproving air. He tried to peer inside her room, but she pulled the door partially closed behind herself so he couldn't.

"I is having a meeting, Daddy. This is importants. It is about loves and wishes. I can't eats dinner yet," she explained in a very serious tone.

Paul studied Morah. She was wearing a pair of oversized golden glasses—without any lens in the frames—one of his white dress shirts unbuttoned down the front, and a name tag with… He tilted his head to read it, Dr. Morah, written in uneven, childish lettering.

"Dr. Morah?" he asked with a raised eyebrow.

She reached up and adjusted her fake glasses and nodded. "The Goddess needs helps. I tolds her if she ever needs helps I would gives it to her. We's having an… inner… inner… a session," she announced with an emphatic nod of her head.

Paul reached out and steadied the tall, pointed princess hat that tilted sideways from her movement. He tried looking into the room again, but Morah pushed a hand against his stomach. He cleared his throat and looked down at her.

"Are you saying you have one of the Goddesses in your bedroom, and you are having an intervention session with her?" he asked.

He wanted to clarify what he was going to tell Morian.

"Yes—and you is interruptings us," Morah pointed out.

"My apologies. I'll let Mommy know you'll be busy for a bit longer," he replied, trying not to laugh.

"Thank you, Daddy," she replied.

She began to close the door before she paused, sniffed the air, looked down the hallway, then turned eyes filled with longing up to him. He could see the conflict on her face. The sound of her tummy rumbling gave her thoughts away.

"How about I bring you a plate—or two. After all, counseling a Goddess is hard work, and I imagine both of you are probably hungry," he suggested.

Morah's face lit up with delight, and she wrapped her arms around his legs. He adjusted her hat again when she pulled back and looked up at him with a smile. He bent down and kissed her forehead.

"I'll put a tray outside the door," he murmured.

"You are the best Daddy evers," she whispered back to him.

As she went back into her bedroom and closed the door, he frowned. Why would a Goddess need help with love issues? More importantly —what was Morah telling her? He jumped with a start when a slender arm wrapped around his waist.

"Is everything alright?" Morian asked, resting her chin against his arm.

"Sometimes I feel very old," he replied with a sigh.

Morian laughed and shook her head. "Trust me when I say I'm the one who robbed the cradle," she teased before she looked at the door and continued, "Please tell me she isn't plotting to take over the world."

He shook his head. "No. She is going to need a tray with dinner for two," he replied, sliding his arm around her as they both walked back to the living room.

"Two?" she inquired with a surprised expression.

He nodded. "It would appear that she is now Dr. Morah, counselor to the Goddesses," he chuckled.

Morian glanced up at him in surprise before looking back over her shoulder. Her lips were parted, and her eyes were wide, so he couldn't resist kissing her.

"Oh my," she replied with a laugh.

"Yes. I suspect this is only the beginning. I'll make her a tray," he said with a shake of his head.

Arosa looked at the little girl as she adjusted the gold, symbiot-created glasses on her nose. Morah smoothed down the white shirt she wore over a glittering pink gown as she resumed her seat on the pink bench.

Arosa wondered for the thousandth time if she should have come here. It had been an impulsive decision to come visit the Valdier palace. She was searching for answers and hoped that perhaps seeing how the older Valdier interacted would give her some guidance.

Instead, she felt more confused than ever. The longing inside her grew stronger as she watched the couples laughing, kissing, and talking with each other. Those moments reminded her of her evening with Tamblin. With still no response from Aikaterina or Arilla, she had sought the only other person who she thought could help her—Morah.

"Okays, where weres we?" Morah asked.

"You were explaining that what I was feeling is love," Arosa replied from where she was lying on Morah's bed.

Morah nodded, almost toppling her princess hat. "Okays. Buttercup, you takes notes this times," she instructed.

Arosa gave the little girl a faint smile when she looked at the symbiot over the rim of her glasses. Buttercup was laying on the floor in the shape of a rabbit. There was a child's tablet lying between the symbiot's paws. Buttercup wiggled her nose and sniffed the tablet.

I think I'm glad that Arilla can't see me now, Arosa ruefully thought.

"Okays, does the Kings of the Leprechaun's makes you mad?" Morah asked.

Arosa frowned and began to sit up. She stopped when Morah gave her a pointed look and shook her head. Leaning back and relaxing against the pile of pillows again, she demurely folded her hands like Morah had instructed earlier and shook her head.

"No. Should he?" she asked.

"Onlys if yous in love like Aunty Riley or likes Springs. They is always threatenings to buries a body. Spring could do it becauses she likes to digs holes. Maybe I should tell Aunty Riley she needs to talks to Spring," Morah responded, tapping a finger to her chin.

"Is that the only way to know if what you feel for someone is love?" Arosa inquired.

Morah shook her head. "No. My mommy and daddy loves each others a lots. They have a quiets love. I thinks that is the kinds of love that you and the Leprechaun has," she decided.

"What do you suggest I do?" Arosa asked.

Morah stood up and walked over to her. She watched with growing apprehension as Morah held her hand and looked at her with a solemn expression. Worried, she sat up.

"You's gots to go to him. Loves is what makes the worlds go round," she said in a low, determined tone.

"But—what do I tell him when he finds out that I'm not really the Queen of the Wood Fairies?" Arosa asked in a hushed voice.

"If he's loves you, it won't matters. My daddy didn't cares that my mommy was a dragon. He loves her because she's my mommy," Morah declared.

Arosa frowned. She wasn't sure it was the same thing—but maybe it was. She lifted a hand to her chest. The strange beating was there again, along with a fluttering in her stomach. Both feelings were alien to her.

"I'll go," she said.

Morah reached over and hugged her. "Don't forgets to tells him the truth. Mommy says if you tells the truth, he's gots to forgive you," she added.

Arosa nodded. "I will. Thank you for your guidance, Little Priestess," she replied.

"Are you hungrys? My daddy was making us some dinner," Morah said.

Arosa shook her head. "No, thank you. I have a few things to do before I go," she said.

"Do you minds if I eat all of your foods? I's starving," Morah said, rubbing her tummy.

"It would be a shame for it to go to waste," she teased.

"Oh, I forgots something! You needs a pretty dress. I have lots of pretty dresses," Morah exclaimed.

Arosa wanted to protest, but the excitement on Morah's face was too much for her tender heart to decline. Ten minutes later, she clutched a beautiful green and silver doll gown to her chest and stepped through an opening back to the Hive.

She solidified and walked along the path, rolling the silky material of the doll gown between her fingers. She looked around the long cavern. While others who came here saw rough stone and boulders, it was an illusion.

She waved her hand and a ripple of gold flowed outward, revealing her home. She brushed her fingers against the polished marble statues of different beings from many places in the universe. The statues moved under her touch. The polished marble floor had designs of different star systems embedded.

She smiled when she saw a new image forming. It reminded her of the power of her species. Young symbiots lounged along the River of Life that streamed out into space through the large Gateway. She looked up at the ceiling. Brilliant colorful ribbons of stars, planets, and nebulas floated overhead.

Along each side, rows of pillars held up the arched ceiling and no longer looked worn or crumbling. The smooth, cream-colored surfaces were now unblemished with age. Behind the columns , unseen by others, were alcoves that gave privacy to those that visited and those that lived here.

She walked over to her own alcove where she enjoyed creating replicas of worlds and the creatures who she imagined would one day live on them. She traced her fingers over the current model she was working on. She smiled when she realized it was very similar to Valdier.

She looked at the table next to the chaise lounge where she had placed an ornate symbiot bracelet with the etchings of a bat in flight. The symbiot was pulsing with light. She hurried over to it and picked up the bracelet.

"Show me," she requested.

Flashes of images poured through the symbiot to her. "Tamblin," she breathed when she saw his tired face.

The symbiot tied to Batty shared the struggle against the poachers. Arosa trembled when she saw time after time Tamblin barely escaping from the traps set by the larger men. She closed her eyes.

"I can't look the other way and ignore them," she whispered.

She retraced her steps to the main cavern. Impatient, she dissolved and soared across to the star chart for Tamblin's small moon. She activated the appropriate gateway and floated up to the platform.

"I'm coming, Tamblin," she said, stepping through the gateway.

CHAPTER FIVE

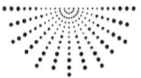

*T*he Minor Moon of Leviathan:

"Batty!" Tamblin yelled as the small bat tumbled from the sky.

He tightened his grip on the saddle as they spiraled downward. He could smell the pungent scent of burned hair. The tiny bat struggled to right himself.

Tamblin cursed when a rock wall came into view in front of them. Batty frantically flapped his wings, but they slammed into the wall. The impact knocked the rider from his perch.

He clung to the saddle, his feet dangling as they slid down the rock face. Tamblin lost his tenuous hold on the saddle when Batty used his thumbs to grip a narrow crevice in the rock.

For a brief second, he was weightless until his feet connected with a ledge. He teetered backwards, his arms flailing outward as he tried to keep his balance. He looked over his shoulder and swallowed. While the ledge he stood on might not be very high for a poacher, it was deadly to someone his size. He twisted and pressed his back against the rock wall behind him.

"I think I got one of them," a man shouted.

Adrenaline poured through him when a bright light flashed in his direction. He crouched down and blindly felt behind him. There was a wide crack in the rock. He slid into it just as the light flashed by him again, illuminating the darkness.

Right inside the entrance there was a hollowed out area. He ducked into it, crouching to keep from hitting his head. The sound of heavy footsteps came closer. He reached down and pulled a knife from his boot.

"Anything yet, Harron?" a man asked.

"No. I could have sworn I hit the creature. Help me find it," Harron replied.

Tamblin flattened his body as far as he could in the narrow gap. A light slowly flashed over the rock. Light danced across the opening, giving him a better view of the cave. It was deeper than he'd expected, going back several feet before widening.

He inhaled a swift breath when the light focused on the crevice where he was hiding. A dirty hand, almost as wide as he was tall, appeared. Tamblin tightened his grip on the knife in his hand.

His breathing grew shallow when long, thick fingers felt around the interior. As long as the man didn't curl his fingers, he should be safe. The man cursed when a jagged piece of rock along the ceiling sliced his flesh. The man would have been able to remove his hand again if he hadn't twisted it.

"What's wrong?" the other man asked.

"My hand's stuck," Harron growled.

"Well, you should have known better than to stick it in there. There's no telling what kind of poisonous creatures might live in the rocks," the other man said with a snicker of amusement.

"Shut up and help me pull my arm out," Harron snapped.

Tamblin lifted an arm to protect his head from falling debris as Harron yanked his arm free. He listened to the two men mutter to each other. Only when the light moved away did he lean his head back and take a deep, calming breath. He stiffly climbed out of his hiding place and stood.

He was taking a step forward when he noticed a movement out of the corner of his eye. He jerked back with a muttered oath, then a soft chuckle of relief slipped from him when Batty peered in the crevice opening at him. The wily creature wiggled until he was through the crack.

"Come, let me look at your wound," he softly instructed.

Remorse filled Tamblin when Batty limped by him to the back of the cave. He followed. He ran his hand along Batty's side to the buckle of the saddle and quickly removed it along with the harness.

Feeling inside the saddlebag, he pulled out a small expanding staff. With a twist, the red gem on the end began to glow. In the light, he could see the dark streak of blood along the bat's side.

He propped the staff up against the wall and reached inside the bag once more, pulling out a small medical kit. He cleaned the wound, whispering soothing words when Batty squeaked in pain. The medicine numbed the area and would prevent infection.

"Thank you, my young friend. If not for you, I would never have seen those men," he confessed.

Batty nudged Tamblin with his head. Compassion filled him when Batty's eyes drooped with fatigue. They both needed some rest. It would be light in a few hours. Although that would make it easier for him to see, it would restrict Batty—and make it more dangerous to travel by air.

He looked up at the ceiling and back down at Batty. "Get some rest," he ordered.

Batty nodded and pushed off the floor of the cavern. He watched the bat gracefully twist in the air and clutch the ceiling with his feet, hanging upside down. In seconds, Batty had wrapped his wings around his body and was sound asleep.

Tamblin returned the items to the bag, sheathed his knife, and walked to the entrance of the cave. He stood there for some time, silently scanning the area. In the distance, he could see the poachers' lights moving away. Depression hit him hard.

"How will we ever win against such odds?" he wondered out loud.

Tia had said that Arosa could help them—but how? Even if she had an army, it would be no match against the poachers and their machines. A shudder ran through him when he remembered the size of the man's hand. One squeeze and the poacher could crush him. He didn't want to think of the damage the man could do to someone as delicate as Arosa.

He looked back into the cave. If he continued on, he might make it to the forest before the end of the day. His decision made, he returned to the back of the cave. He packed a smaller bag with a few essentials and pulled the strap over his head.

Batty's squeak caused him to look up. Large brown and gold eyes gaze down at him with an accusing expression. A wave of remorse swept through him. It was obvious Batty thought he was abandoning him.

"I will continue on. Find me when nightfall comes again. I want you healthy and well-rested," he gently instructed, picking up the staff.

Batty wiggled his nose and blinked in response before nodding and covering his head with his wing again. With his guilt slightly eased, Tamblin tightened the strap to the bag on his back and strode back to the opening. He took a deep breath and began descending the rock face. He still had a long, treacherous journey ahead of him.

Arosa solidified on the edge of the rock shelf in front of a dark cave. Her symbiot connection with the young bat had guided her to his location. Behind her, the sun was rising above the horizon.

"Tamblin," she called, stepping up to the cave's entrance. She lifted a hand and a golden light filtered from it into the opening. "Tamblin, are you hurt?" she anxiously asked, hurrying forward.

She stopped when she saw the saddle. She peered up at the ceiling. Batty unfurled his wings, yawned, and looked down at her with sleepy eyes.

"Batty, where is Tamblin?" she asked in an urgent tone.

She floated up to the bat and caressed his head with a gentle hand. Her breath caught when she sensed Batty's pain. The bat looked at her with sad eyes.

"Show me," she coaxed.

Batty lifted his left wing, showing her a long burn, blistered and red, on his side. She ran her hand along the wound. The flesh sealed and fine, dark brown hair grew as she caressed the damaged area. She murmured soothing words when the small bat trembled.

"Where is Tamblin?" she asked.

"I will continue on. Find me when nightfall comes again. I want you healthy and well-rested." Tamblin's deep voice echoed through her mind.

"No!" she cried, looking back toward the crevice opening.

Twirling, she floated out of the cavern. Power flowed through her as her fear for Tamblin grew. She reached out, connecting with every living being—both plant and animal. A vision of Tamblin appeared. He was running, and she noticed the lines under the ground moving behind him—sandworms.

She burst forward and in a matter of seconds, she located him. The ground under his feet rose, sending him flying. He hit the ground and rolled, coming up onto his feet with a long staff in his hand. He swung around as three sandworms broke through the surface and surrounded him.

She opened her arms, shifting into the Wood Fairy Queen, and wrapped her arms around his waist from behind. She lifted him off the ground as two of the sandworms struck, flying up to the top of a mushroom, and released him. Turning in midair, she swept her hands outward. The sandworms' bodies rippled as they began to change. Their bodies became stems, and their open mouths turned into dark red flowers with yellow and orange centers.

"Arosa!" Tamblin exclaimed in shock, sheathing his sword.

"A beast is coming. It isn't safe for you out in the open," she said.

She swept her arms around him again and lifted him off the mushroom, depositing him onto the ground. He gripped her hand, and they ran through the maze of mushrooms—until the ground suddenly gave way under his feet.

Arosa twisted when Tamblin's hand unexpectedly ripped away from hers. She realized that a sandworm tunnel had opened under his feet. Terror gripped her when he disappeared. She faded again, reappearing next to him as he fell.

She wrapped her arms around him, and with a thought, a thick pile of soft spores appeared under them. They landed on the cushioned floor of the tunnel. The impact forced them apart.

"Arosa, are you alright?" Tamblin urgently asked.

She sat up and sneezed. She lifted her eyes to his and choked back a giggle. A dusting of fine, rainbow-colored particles covered Tamblin from head to foot.

"I'm fine. Are you hurt?" she asked, grasping his hand when he held it out.

He grimaced when he saw his clothing. "Only my pride," he chuckled, brushing the colorful powder off of his clothing.

They both looked up when the ground shook and pieces of dirt rained down. Tamblin lifted her out of the pile of spores, pulled her away from the opening, and held her in his arms. She pressed against him and looked over her shoulder.

"Did the beast find something this time, Macron?" a man shouted.

"Maybe. There's a hole," Macron answered.

Arosa looked at Tamblin. He shook his head. She pressed her face against him when the sound of savage snarling reverberated around them. The snarls were followed by a cascade of dirt as the ground was ripped opened. Long, sharp claws dug at the soil. The beast was enlarging the hole they had fallen through.

"This way," Tamblin murmured near her ear.

CHAPTER SIX

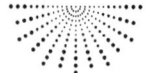

*O*nce he determined it was safe, Tamblin twisted the crystal at top of his staff. Its red glow lit the sandworm tunnel. The last thing he wanted to do was to run face first into one of those beasts. He was conscious of Arosa's tight grip on the back of his coat.

"Where are we going?" she inquired.

He glanced over his shoulder before focusing on where he was going. It was a good thing he did because he would have run face first into a long root hanging from the tunnel ceiling. He reached out and pushed it out of the way, holding it back until Arosa passed through.

"We are searching for another way out," he explained.

He stopped and looked up when the ground above them shook. The loud sound of a creature sniffing sent a shiver through him. He reached back and gripped Arosa's hand, pulling her quickly behind him when the creature growled.

When the tunnel collapsed, they were only a few feet away. From the opening above, light poured in, and a narrow beige-colored snout appeared. Long, sharp teeth protruded from the beast's mouth, and the creature's massive claws tore at the ground.

"Macron, call your beast off! At the rate it's going, we're going to have a trench, and it will have eaten anything worth selling," a poacher snapped in irritation.

"Shut up, Harron. If we want to make this trip worthwhile, we're going to need more than the Tasiers. We'll be lucky if we get enough credits to pay for the fuel for this disaster, and if the Dragon Lords find out what we're doing, we'll be lucky to make it out of here alive. You saw the sensors. If the blockers we put on them fail and it sends out a report, we're dead," Macron retorted.

"What are they trying to do?" Arosa asked.

Tamblin paused when the tunnel forked. He lifted the staff and looked at each tunnel before he turned to the right. He kept a tight grip on Arosa's hand as they moved farther away from the poachers and their beast.

"Tia had a vision that the poachers would return to our moon. My security teams sighted the first of them a few weeks ago. They set out traps to capture the Tasiers," he explained, stopping to look up at one narrow hole.

"But—the Valdier have declared this moon under their protection," she protested.

Tamblin nodded. "Yes, but they aren't here. Our hope was the sensors the Valdier scientists installed would trigger an alert and bring help, but as you just heard, the poachers have blocked them," he replied, continuing along the passage.

"Why are they trying to capture you? You are not a Tasier," she demanded.

He stopped and faced her. In the staff's glow, he could see the worry and confusion on her face. He brushed a smudge of dirt from her cheek.

"We have been trying to disable their ships and release Tasiers from their traps for the past month," he said.

"Oh, Tamblin, I'm so sorry," she replied, cupping his hand against her cheek.

He shook his head. "For the first few days, we were successful, but the poachers soon discovered there was something amiss. They repaired their ships almost as fast as we could sabotage them. Then they set traps for us. Several warriors were injured, and we almost lost a team when they became trapped on board a transport. Jett and Santil freed them at the last second. We continued releasing the Tasiers, but even that became too hazardous to do during the daylight hours. For the next couple of weeks, squadrons worked at night, but the poachers upgraded the locking mechanisms. We could no longer open the traps as quickly as before. Then, a creature like the one we encountered back there caught one of our soldiers—and nearly killed him. We rescued him but not before a poacher saw us. Now, those two hunt us as much as they do the Tasiers. Roan, King of Sandora, and I have both sent scouts out to warn other kingdoms," he said.

"And you came looking for me," she replied.

"Yes. Everyone on the moon is in danger, including the Wood Fairies. I wanted to find you earlier, to find out why you disappeared the next morning without saying goodbye—It doesn't matter. I shouldn't have brought that up now." He looked away from her.

"Tamblin—"

"We'd best keep moving," he said, walking away.

He tried to ignore the hurt in her eyes. He was just trying to protect his own heart from being hurt again. Her disappearance the morning after their night together had been like a dagger to his heart. She had vanished, leaving nothing behind but a note attached to Batty.

"Tamblin," she called from behind him.

He slowed his pace, realizing he had been so focused on his thoughts that he wasn't paying attention. He took a deep breath and faced her. He frowned when she didn't walk toward him.

"What?" he asked in a tone sharper than he meant. "I'm sorry, Arosa. What is it?"

She pointed to a tunnel. His frown deepened, and he walked over to her. The passage made a gradual incline and opened at the base of an outcropping of rocks.

"I thought this might be a good exit," she softly replied.

He cleared his throat and nodded. "Yes, it's perfect. I'll go first to make sure it's safe," he said.

Arosa stared at Tamblin's back with longing. She had created the tunnel, knowing it would give them safe passage to the surface. Lifting the hem of her dress, she followed him at a slower pace.

Remorse filled her. He was hurt by her sudden disappearance that night, of course he was. She hadn't known how to handle all the unfamiliar emotions sweeping through her then, and she still didn't.

What future could we ever have? she thought.

"It's safe," he said, holding out his hand to her.

She placed her hand in his and climbed up the steep incline. He helped her out of the hole, and they scrambled to hide behind the rocks. A hundred yards away, two large poachers stood talking while a hairless mammal with a long and wrinkled snout, beady black eyes, and stubby ears clawed at the ground. The beast's head disappeared in the hole and when it reemerged, a torn piece of her gown hung from between its teeth.

A man's shout of triumph split the air as he yanked the cloth from the beast's mouth. He waved it in the other man's face. She and Tamblin ducked their heads when the man looked around.

"I told you I saw something!" Macron chortled.

Harron grabbed the material and turned it over in his hand before he tossed it back at Macron. "That's a dress for a doll," he retorted in disgust.

"Hey now, do you see any kids around here? I'm telling you it belongs to those creatures that are sabotaging our ships and releasing the Tasiers," Macron argued.

"The only one who saw something was you, and I made the mistake of believing your wild tales. We need to focus on the Tasiers. We haven't lost any more of them since we upgraded the locks on the traps—that *I* purchased, I might add. How do I know you aren't trying to jeopardize this business endeavor?" Harron sneered.

Macron grabbed Harron by the collar, and the two men struggled for a few minutes. Arosa stared at the conflict with a combination of awe and horror. She jumped when Tamblin wrapped his fingers around her arm.

"Why are they fighting with each other?" she asked.

Tamblin frowned. "Because that is what they do," he replied.

She lifted the hem of the green and silver gown Morah had given her and followed him as he climbed. She gazed up at the mountain of rocks. This was a lot more work than she'd expected.

"Where are we going?" she asked with a sigh.

Tamblin stopped and looked over his shoulder at her. "First, we are going to find a place where we are safe. Then, we are going to head back to my kingdom," he explained, resuming his climb.

"But—why are we heading north if your kingdom is to the east?" she asked.

He stopped. She stared at his stiff frame. His shoulders rose and fell as if he were taking a deep breath, holding it, and then releasing it.

"I was coming to find you because Tia said you had the power to save our world—and she is never wrong. Now, we are returning to the cave where I left Batty, which is north of here," he replied.

Arosa swayed with shock. "Tia told you about me?" she asked.

Tamblin looked over his shoulder at her again and frowned. "I told her that unless you have an army we don't know about, I find it very unlikely that you can help us, but I have a duty to my people to try anything I can to save them. If you can turn the poachers into flowers the way you did the sandworms, that would work," he replied with a raised eyebrow.

She shook her head. "I—can't," she said, biting her lip.

He sighed. "Well, I guess that was too much to hope for. We'd better move. Once they finish beating each other up, they'll start searching for us again," he replied.

Arosa nodded, not that Tamblin saw the movement. He had already turned around and started climbing again. She tried to follow him, but her feet kept slipping on the loose gravel.

She sighed and looked down at her feet. This terrain required more practical footwear than the slippers she was wearing. In the blink of an eye, the dainty slippers were transformed into a pair of sturdy hiking boots. She lifted the gown and secured it with a wide, golden belt that appeared around her waist.

With a flutter of her wings, she rose off the ground. Tamblin was a fair distance from her now, and flying would be the fastest—and easiest—way to catch up with him.

As soon as she was close to him, she squeaked in surprise when he swiftly turned, wrapped his arm around her waist, and pulled her down against his body. She tried to speak, but he covered her mouth with his hand and stared over her shoulder. He muttered a curse and frantically searched the area around them.

"Stay quiet. They are coming this way," he warned, pulling her down until she was crouching beside him.

She nodded when he moved his hand. He kept his arms wrapped around her as they peered between the rocks. Her flight up to Tamblin must have attracted the men's attention.

"You busted my nose," Macron growled, wiping the blood off with the sleeve of his shirt.

"You bit me," Harron retorted. "What is it?"

Macron stopped a few feet from Tamblin and Arosa. "I saw something," he remarked in a distracted voice.

Tamblin held her tighter when Macron took another step closer. Arosa narrowed her eyes and focused on the ground. Hundreds of small butterflies rose from the mushrooms and swarmed around the two men. She lifted her hand and smothered her giggles when the men jumped back with startled yells.

When she looked at the hairless beast, she noticed that it was staring in their direction. A mischievous smile curved her lips.

Do not hunt the Tasiers or the people of this moon any longer. They are under my protection, she instructed.

The hairless beast bowed its head. It turned, looked at the two men dancing in frantic circles before it took off in the direction of the ships. The men soon followed the beast. Satisfied with her ploy, she leaned back and beamed when Tamblin softly chuckled in her ear.

"Maybe this is why Tia said I needed to find you," he mused.

"Why is that?" she asked, looking at him.

She caught her breath when their lips nearly touched. She stared into his eyes as a heightened sense of awareness flooded her. He tightened his hold on her.

"Luck—perhaps you will bring us luck," he replied.

She parted her lips and leaned into him, hoping he would kiss her. Disappointment quickly replaced anticipation when he rose to his feet, pulling her up with him. He released her and stepped back.

"We'd better go. It will take us a few days to get back to Glitter. A laser blast hit Batty. I left him in a cave a half day's journey from here. If possible, I'd like to get back to him before dark," he said, avoiding her eyes.

She silently nodded, not bothering to hide the hurt caused by his rejection. Instead, she followed him down the rocks to the ground. It didn't seem necessary to inform him that Batty was safe and his wounds now healed. He would discover that when they reached the cave.

CHAPTER SEVEN

*T*amblin paused and looked over his shoulder at Arosa. She wiped her damp brow and gave him a quivering smile. He looked away from her and scanned the area.

"We can take a break here," he said.

She silently followed him. He stopped under an enormous red and yellow mushroom with soft white gills. Dozens of smaller mushrooms grew under the protective umbrella of the larger one. He shrugged off his coat and covered the top of one of the smaller mushrooms.

"You can sit here. This way you won't ruin your dress," he offered.

"Thank you, but I think it is a little late for that," she ruefully replied, fingering a long tear in the green material.

A surge of shame over his behavior threatened to swallow him. He'd spent the last two hours fluctuating between wanting to wrap his arms around her and being a total jerk. It happened that being a total jerk had won.

She swept her damp hair back and sighed, pointedly looking at everything except him. He placed his pack on the ground and retrieved his water bottle. He shook it, muttering under his breath when he realized it was empty.

"Do you need water?" she asked.

He nodded. "We need water. It is important we stay hydrated," he replied as he stood.

She worried her bottom lip. "If you like, I can—"

He shook his head. "I've got this," he interrupted and removed the knife from his boot.

She loudly sighed and became quiet again. He looked around the area, sending up a silent thank you to the Goddesses when he saw the flat, ruffled texture of a milk-white Dragon's Beard mushroom.

The Dragon's Beard would not only give them plenty of water, but its meat was sweet, delicious, and nutritious. He walked over to the plant and poked a small hole in it with his knife. Clear water poured from it into the bottle. When it was full, he cut a small section off the tip of the mushroom.

In seconds, a thin film covered the cut section, sealing off the flow of water and protecting the mushroom. He carried the mushroom piece and the water back to Arosa and held out the bottle. She gave him a brief smile before she took the offered bottle of water.

"Thank you," she said.

He studied her when she stared at the bottle before sniffing it. An amused smile tugged at his lips when she finally took a drink. She seemed almost surprised by the cool liquid. She drank deeply before sighing again.

"There is plenty more," he assured her.

She shook her head and offered him the bottle. "You have some first. You have been traveling longer than I," she insisted.

He took the bottle and sat down beside her. Placing the bottle between his legs, he tore the piece of mushroom and handed half of it to her.

She fingered the soft white meat before pinching off a section and placing it in her mouth.

"This is good," she remarked with surprise.

"Do you not have Dragon's Beard in your forest?" he asked before breaking off a section and eating it.

"This type of fungi is found on many planets, though they call it different names. Aik—" she started to explain before she stopped and looked at the piece in her hand. "It is very good," she finished lamely.

"How did you find me earlier?" he suddenly asked.

She choked on a small piece of mushroom she was eating and coughed. He patted her on the back and handed her the water bottle. She took a deep swig and cleared her throat.

"I… the butterflies warned that there was a disturbance and I…uh… came to investigate," she haltingly answered.

"I'm thankful that you did. It was interesting how you could do that— turn the sandworms into flowers," he reflected.

"It… as the Queen of the Wood Fairies, I have a certain skill when it comes to plants. The sandworms weren't harmed. The flowers grew around them," she said with a wave of her hand.

"Fascinating," he murmured.

"It is? Yes, it is," she hastily corrected.

He wanted to ask her one more question that was puzzling him—*why had she left him without saying goodbye the morning after*—but he was afraid of the answer. There was a lot he wanted to say, but an awkward silence fell between them as they finished their simple meal. He offered her the bottle again.

"No, thank you," she said, wiping the mushroom crumbs off her dress.

"I'll refill the water bottle and cut another section off the mushroom just in case we need it later. It tastes better roasted. We should get going if we want to make it back to Batty by nightfall. I told him to find me, but I don't know if he understood. He might end up back at the palace," he mused.

"He understood," she replied.

She looked so certain he couldn't help asking, "How can you be certain?"

She gave him that mysterious smile of hers and slid off the mushroom. "Bats are very smart creatures," she replied with a confident nod.

"Well, I think we should still try to get back to the cave. If nothing else, it will give us protection. The poachers are more active at night," he said.

He refilled the water bottle and cut off another piece of the mushroom. She held his bag and coat while he stored their meager supplies. The tiny frown line between her eyes made him smile. She was watching everything he did as if it were all new to her.

Her soft cheek was smudged with dirt. He took his coat from her and pulled a handkerchief from the pocket. Dampening one end with the trickle of water still dripping from the mushroom, he gently wiped the spot.

"Tamblin," she whispered, looking at him, her eyes filled with longing and confusion.

He caressed her cheek with his thumb. "We'd better go," he quietly responded.

After several stops, they reached the bottom of the rock face where he had left Batty just before dusk. The last couple of hours had been the most taxing. He had pushed not only himself but Arosa at an exhausting pace. His biggest motivation was fear for her. The thought of her being exposed to the horrors of the poachers superseded everything else.

He held out his hand. "Just a little farther, we are almost there," he promised.

She grasped his hand and stepped up beside him on a rock. "I can take us the rest of the way," she offered.

The protest on his lips died when she wrapped her arms around him. She looked up at the opening, and when he looked up too, his feet left the ground. Her wings fluttered so quickly he barely saw them. In seconds, they were on the ledge from where he had descended nearly fourteen hours earlier.

"Thank—thank you," he said when she released him.

She self-consciously pushed a lock of her hair back and gave him a shy smile. "You're welcome," she replied before walking past him into the cave.

He followed her with his gaze until she disappeared from sight. He sighed and looked behind him at the horizon. Bright spotlights and the unmistakably gray clouds of smoke created a glowing haze along the skyline.

Hopelessness filled him as he stared out at the devastation. These men cared nothing about the lives they were destroying. Their only concern was for the credits they would earn.

Tia, I fear nothing short of a Goddess can save our world this time, he thought with despair.

CHAPTER EIGHT

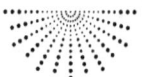

*A*rosa glanced over her shoulder before studying the cave in front of her. Batty peeked down at her and gave her a toothy grin at the changes she made to the drab interior. All day she had fought against the urge to make things easier for Tamblin.

Even so, she might have been responsible for the Dragon Beard mushrooms appearing when they needed water... and because of her, no sandworms tried to attack them. Also, there had been a cooling breeze that stayed with them, there were fewer obstacles to block their way, and heavy rain had kept the poachers from the area.

Now she focused on making the night more pleasant. The cave expanded. In the corner, a deep oval depression formed. Water poured down along the wall from a crack and filled the area, then the torrent became a continuous trickle. In another corner, dried wood appeared. There would be enough firewood for several nights.

Batty squeaked in appreciation. She sent him a mischievous glance and lifted a finger to her lips. She smiled and the ceiling of the cave came alive with glowing green lights from iridescent glow worms.

"Don't eat them. They are merely an illusion," she cautioned.

Tamblin would need something to sleep on—but what could she add that would look natural? She worried her bottom lip as she scanned the area. An idea formed, and long, soft curly moss grew down from the ceiling, forming thick clumps next to the pool of water. The moss flowed outward until it created a level area on the floor.

This will work, she decided with satisfaction.

Batty squeaked again and landed next to her. She scratched behind his ear when he pressed his head against her side.

Tamblin stepped into the larger section of the cavern and Batty's eyes lit up with pleasure. Tamblin affectionately murmured to Batty when he scurried over to Tamblin with a joyous squeak.

"He missed you," she teased.

Tamblin chuckled and stroked Batty. "He *is* an affectionate creature. I've never seen one behave like this," he admitted. He looked around the cavern. "I don't remember the cave looking like this before."

"You said it was dark when you left," she reminded him.

The confusion in his eyes faded, and he nodded. "True. I'll admit I'm glad it is much nicer than I remembered," he confessed.

"Batty can keep watch for us. I believe I saw some wood in the corner. Do you have a way to light a fire?" she asked.

Tamblin nodded and frowned again. "I must have been more exhausted or distracted than I realized. I know Batty was hurt. I remember applying salve to his wound, but there's no mark. Even his hair has grown back," he mused.

She nervously shifted when Tamblin ran his hand along the bat's side where he'd been wounded. Batty looked at her with wide eyes, as if trying to decide if he should squeak in pain. She frantically nodded, trying not to laugh when Batty overdramatized his pain, fell over onto his other side, and covered his head with his wing.

"On second thought, maybe he's hurt worse than I realized," Tamblin said.

"If you'd like to start a fire, I will tend to Batty," she offered.

He reluctantly nodded. "I hope he doesn't have any broken ribs."

"I'm sure he is fine. Perhaps a little sore still," she reassured him.

She flashed Tamblin a brief, encouraging smile when he nodded again and walked away. Batty peeked at her from under his wing. She barely smothered her chuckle of amusement when she noticed the mischievous delight reflected in the bat's eyes and he winked.

"Thank you," she murmured.

She distractedly stroked Batty's side while she watched Tamblin work. He was meticulous. He thought out each of his movements before he did them, paying attention to every detail.

Before long, he had a fire burning in a small pit. She was curious when she noticed that he anchored two sticks in the pile of rocks until he pulled out the remaining pieces of mushroom from his bag. He washed them before skewering and securing them over the fire to roast.

"He makes doing the simplest things fascinating," she mused.

As if he heard her, he looked up and their eyes connected. Her hand skimmed along Batty's wing as she took a step, then two toward Tamblin. Batty, sensing it was time to go, rolled to his feet and scurried toward the cave entrance.

"If you'd like to get cleaned up, dinner will be ready soon," Tamblin informed her.

"What about you?" she asked.

He chuckled. "It wouldn't hurt for me to get cleaned up as well," he acknowledged.

"Good," she said, reaching for him.

She covered his lips with hers in a passionate kiss. He stiffened with surprise and then moaned as he wrapped his arms around her. The hammering in her chest increased and excitement coursed through her.

"Arosa," he groaned, kissing her neck.

"Yes, Tamblin. Yes," she replied, unfastening his shirt.

An hour later, Tamblin kissed Arosa's bare shoulder where her gown had slipped down. Memories of the magic they had just created in the shallow pool burned through his mind, making him hungry for more. Her giggle caused him to smile.

"We're lucky the food didn't burn," he said, handing her one of the sticks with a section of the roasted mushroom on it.

"Yes, we are," she responded.

"Why did you leave?" he suddenly asked, sitting down across from her.

She gave him a startled look and lowered her eyes. He watched a variety of expressions cross her face as she thought about how to answer him. She picked at the mushroom.

"Tamblin, there is something I should have told you," she began.

The sound of Batty's frantic squeaking interrupted her. He placed his meal aside and stood, grabbing his shirt and pulling it on as he hurried to the entrance of the cave. The bright glow of fires stretched out to the horizon. The acrid stench of smoke filled the air. Fastening his shirt, he skidded to a stop beside Batty.

"Goddess, no!" he exclaimed in horror at the sight before him.

The poachers must have realized they were running out of time. Fires scorched the moon for as far as he could see. Dozens of poachers on skimmers drove the Tasiers into massive traps. What horrified him the most was that in the distance there was a machine drilling into the side of a mountain—his mountain—the home of the Kingdom of Glitter.

CHAPTER NINE

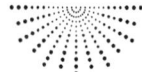

"Faster, Batty," Tamblin encouraged, leaning low over the bat's neck.

Arosa clung to his waist. Batty quivered with fear as the flames rose, creating a turbulent current of superheated air. Tamblin's eyes burned from the smoke. He leaned to the left when a poacher's skimmer came into view.

His fury intensified when he saw the man aim his flamethrower at the ground. He could see terrified Tasiers scurrying for safety while the man laughed. A feeling of helplessness overcame him at his inability to stop the alien.

Goddess, if you can hear me, please help us, he silently pleaded.

As if the Goddess had heard his request, the flame glowing at the end of the flamethrower's wand sputtered and went out. It was a fleeting moment of salvation for the poor Tasiers still running for their lives.

With that prayer answered, Tamblin looked toward the mountain ahead. He choked back his cry of rage when the tip of the drill bit disappeared into the rock. It looked like it might have broken through to the main chamber. His worst fears were confirmed when hundreds of mounted bats and sand skimmers emerged.

"Arosa, can you fly?" he urgently demanded.

"Yes," she breathlessly replied.

"I will get you as close as I can. I need you to find Tia and Arielle. Please make sure they get to safety," he instructed.

"Tamblin," she began.

He covered her hand with his and squeezed it. "Please. My people will need somewhere to go. Your kingdom may be our only hope," he said before he released her hand and pulled on Batty's rein. "Go!"

He gritted his teeth to keep from calling out to her when she rose behind him. Pressing his heels into Batty's side, he urged the bat forward. He pulled the staff from the pouch on the saddle and twisted the end. It seemed like a feeble defense against such overwhelming odds, but the power crystal and the remaining guardians were the only weapons available.

Arosa floated in the air, watching with growing horror and sadness. The loud shout of triumph from the poacher on the drilling machine drew the attention of his cohorts in crime. She recognized him as the one called Macron. The bright flares from the Leviathan warriors did little more than cause Macron to swear in a loud voice.

"Harron, fire the nets! Fire the nets!" Macron shouted.

Harron fired a weapon that sent a net over the opening, preventing any more warriors from flying out of the gaping hole the drill had created. She flew forward when a warrior was knocked off of his skimmer.

She wrapped her arms around the falling rider. Slender arms clung to her in shock. Arosa landed on an outcropping of rock a safe distance from the battle.

"Thank you, Goddess," a soft voice shakily said.

"Tia! What are you doing here? What has happened?" she anxiously asked.

Tia reached up and removed her helmet. A trickle of blood ran from a cut on her temple. Arosa looked into Tia's haunted eyes.

"Our home—my people—our world...." Tia incoherently said, looking around her before she continued, "We need your help, Goddess. Please —for the sake of my people, my daughter, Jett... and Tamblin, I beg you to help us."

Arosa swallowed and followed Tia's gaze. Aikaterina always said they were only to observe. But, hadn't Aikaterina helped the Valdier and other species when she gave them symbiots and the abilities to shift and harness their surrounding energy? Hadn't Aminta given gifts to each of the rulers of the Seven Kingdoms to guide and protect them?

How could she stand by and watch the destruction of this world when she had the power to save it? What was the purpose of having such power, if not to use it for good? As the questions and doubts assailed her, she realized that she would give up everything to protect this world and the man that she had fallen in love with—for life and her existence held no meaning otherwise.

"I was dishonest with him. I should have told him who I was," she said.

"He will forgive you," Tia promised.

She looked at Tia. A strange dampness blurred her vision, and she could feel it coursing down her cheeks. She wiped it away with her fingers.

"Tears... I didn't know we could cry," she confessed, looking at the moisture.

"You'll help us?" Tia asked, reaching for her hand.

Arosa closed her fingers around Tia's slender green hand. Her gaze remained fixed on Tamblin. He was trying to slice through a net that had entrapped dozens of warriors while Batty distracted the poacher nearby.

"Yes, I will help. I promised Tamblin that I would make sure that you and your daughter were safe first," she replied.

Tia's startled protest ended on a growl of frustration when Arosa opened a portal that would take Tia safely back to her daughter. Arosa smiled faintly. Now that her promise to Tamblin had been kept, she would keep the one she had made to Tia—regardless of the consequences.

"ENOUGH! This world is under my protection," she commanded.

As her command spread, Arosa grew larger. The illusion of her persona as the Queen of the Wood Fairies faded. Creatures large and small trembled when they saw the power of her natural form. She raised her arms and sent a wave of energy so powerful that the moon trembled and the ships in orbit lost power.

"Forget about the Dragon Lords killing us, Macron. We've gone and angered the Goddesses," Harron whispered in a hoarse voice.

CHAPTER TEN

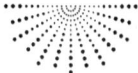

*T*amblin lost his balance and fell sideways when the line he was cutting through gave way. He was about to start on the next cable when the sound of Arosa's voice swept through him as if she were standing next to him. He braced his hand against the ground and looked around.

A shockwave of disbelief passed through him when he saw her. He rose unsteadily to his feet as the image of her as the Queen of the Wood Fairies faded, and in her place was a powerful, larger-than-life Goddess. He dropped down to one knee and bowed his head when she looked in his direction.

"Tamblin," she softly called.

He looked up at her before bowing his head again, curling his fingers into fists as he tried to comprehend what was happening. A movement to his left drew his attention. The net that had pinned the struggling warriors to the ground dissolved.

The faint sound of awe and hushed reverence washed through him. All around him, the poachers' nets turned to ash. The huge aliens dropped to their knees and bowed their heads.

"Goddess, we… uh… we were just… uh…," Macron stuttered.

"I know what you were doing. You were being… horrible," she snapped.

Despite his own sense of intimidation at seeing Arosa in this form and realizing who and what she was, he couldn't help being both proud and amused. Unable to resist, he raised his head and watched Arosa as she glided across the ground to the drilling machine Macron was sitting on. With a snap of her fingers, it vanished and the large male hit the ground.

"If you or any of your kind *ever* come back to this moon, harm or capture another Tasier, or even *think* of harming the species that live here, I swear it will be more than your drilling machine that disintegrates—it will be your spaceship while you are on it or worse! They are *under my protection*! Do you understand?" she demanded.

"Yes, ma'am. I mean, yes, Goddess. We'll never touch another Tasier or come to this place or anywhere near here again," Macron hastily promised.

"I won't either, Goddess," Harron swore.

"You will return every single Tasier that you took off of this moon, and if you find any others, you are to give them to the Valdier who will bring them here," she instructed.

"All of them…," Macron complained before he clamped his lips together when Harron elbowed him.

"We'll return them all, Goddess," Harron promised.

"That's a lot of credits. I mean, if we could keep…," Macron grumbled.

Arosa appeared in front of Macron. Tamblin winced when the man was yanked up off the ground and suspended in midair in front of her. Even in the early morning light, he could see the sweat beading on the alien's brow.

"I don't have to make you disappear all at once. I could start with one piece at a time. So what is more important, credits or—" Arosa paused and ran her furious eyes down over Macron's body before stopping at his crotch.

Several men next to Tamblin winced and snickered under their breath. "I'd pay an alien's credit to have her do it," one warrior chuckled.

He bit back his own laugh when Macron dropped his hands and covered the spot she was eyeing. Even some of the poachers snickered with amusement. After several seconds, she sneered and with a flick her wrist, Macron disappeared.

"Who wishes to be next?" she demanded, glancing over the cowering group of men with a regal stance. "You have one hour to return all the Tasiers to this world. The Valdier will ensure that you miss none of them."

Tamblin and the others of his kind stood and watched with a combination of relief and awe as the poachers hastily departed back to their transports. A hush fell over the group closest to him when Arosa looked at him.

He was trying to think of what to say to her when the world around him changed and he was suddenly in the cave they'd left earlier. He swayed and lifted a hand to his head. A slender arm wrapped around his waist when his knees almost gave out.

"I'm sorry. I used a little too much power. I'm not used to carrying others," she said in an apologetic tone.

He shook his head and immediately regretted it. A low moan slipped from him, and he sat down heavily on the bed that appeared under him. He dropped his hand to the royal blue silk covers.

"This… is a little out of place, don't you think?" he asked with a wry smile.

"Is it? I supposed it is," she ruefully replied, sitting down beside him.

He breathed deeply to calm his wildly beating heart and looked around. Arosa had indeed taken them back to the cave. It was the same —except for the bed.

He brushed his hand against hers and she glanced at him shyly, covertly brushing her fingers against his. He turned her hand over and caressed her palm with his thumb. She had taken the shape of the Fairy Queen.

"Why didn't you tell me who you really were?" he asked in a quiet voice.

"I wanted to, but I was afraid," she confessed.

He quickly looked up at her face and frowned. "You—afraid? Did you see how those huge aliens reacted to you? You made one dissolve with a snap of your fingers," he said in an incredulous tone.

She gave him a crooked smile. "Disappear—I sent him back to his ship in space. I wouldn't actually hurt him. Well, I could, but I would rather not if possible. Several Valdier warships have arrived, and they are searching the ships. I thought it would be good for him to have to face them," she confessed.

Tamblin considered Arosa's contrite expression and shook his head. "Why were you afraid?" he asked.

"How was I supposed to tell the man I fell in love with that I'm considered a Goddess on many worlds? How do I tell him that I'm older than the moon he calls home and as old as the star system he lives in? What was I supposed to tell him—" she said before he cut her off by capturing her lips in a passionate kiss.

She parted her lips, and he deepened the kiss. He slid his arms around her and pulled her down until she was lying on top of him. She wrapped her hands around his neck, her mouth moving against his.

When she rolled her hips against him, he broke the kiss, breathing heavily. Her swollen lips beckoned him for more. She looked nothing like the Goddess and everything like the woman he had fallen in love with, yet, he could see power in her unguarded eyes—the reflection of the universe… and love.

"You tell him just the way you did. I love you for you, Arosa. I love that you are kind and loving—and can scare away the bad guys with the snap of your fingers. I love you for who you are—here," he said, lifting his hand and laying it over her heart. "I hope you can love me the same way. I am but a simple King of a very small but proud species living in a cave on an isolated moon in a vast universe."

"You're perfect, Tamblin," she replied, bowing her head and capturing his lips again.

EPILOGUE

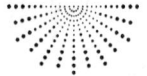

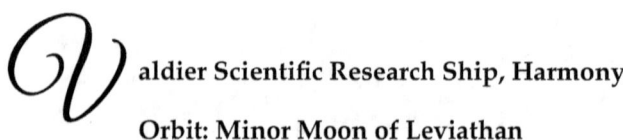 aldier Scientific Research Ship, Harmony:

Orbit: Minor Moon of Leviathan

Mandra Reykill absently listened to the list of items the Harmony's Science Officer, Bale, was relaying to him. His attention was focused on his mate, who was growling—literally—at some unfortunate soul. He stepped through the door into the cargo hold and stopped.

She beautiful when she angry, his dragon growled with delight.

Yes, she is, Mandra agreed with a sigh.

Cages, stacked from floor to ceiling in rows of twenty, filled the cargo hold. Frightened, squeaking Tasiers filled nearly half of the units. However, it wasn't the Tasiers that captured his full attention; it was the beautiful rose and gold dragon snarling at a group of four Qualin poachers who had their hands high in the air. Given the guns on the floor, they seemed to have made the right decision to surrender. Leave it to his mate to find the poachers' stash before the rest of his men did.

Two of his guards standing on each side of Ariel bowed their heads in his direction.

"What have you found out so far, *mi elila*?" Mandra asked, walking over to her.

Ariel's dragon form shimmered and she shifted back into her two-legged form. "I found out that these pieces of trash violated the restrictions regarding this moon and poached a protected species," she replied with a glare at the men.

"Hel... p. Please, someone hel...p me!" a pitiful voice called from one of the cages.

Mandra frowned and scanned the cages. Inside one was a shivering Qualin with ice crystals hanging from his nose. His knees were pressed to his chin in the narrow confines of the metal box, and his clothing was stiff as if frozen.

"He looks like he just came out of the freezer!" Ariel exclaimed.

"Get him out," Mandra ordered with a wave of his hand to Bale and another Valdier warrior.

The two men climbed the cages to the one on top. It took them several minutes, and a cutting tool, to open the cage. When they did, they had to pull the half-frozen man out by his legs and carefully bring him down to the deck with the help of two of the Qualin crew.

"What is your name and explain what happened," Mandra demanded.

The man tried to lift his chin, but he couldn't, so he just looked up. "M-Ma... cron, my... Lord. The G-God...d-dess," Macron stuttered.

Surprise swept through Mandra before he began to chuckle. Ariel and Bale looked at him with a curious expression. He shook his head. He knew exactly how mischievous the Goddesses could be. The last time, they had shrunk him, his brothers, and his extended family while on a camping trip—all so the kids could go on an adventure to find the King of the Leprechauns!

"Yes, well, by order of the Valdier, this moon is a protected habitat. We allow no one to harvest, sell, or harm any of the Tasiers or other inhabitants," Mandra stated.

"You... you don't have... to worry about me... *ever* coming back, my Lord. That... the Goddess threatened... to dissolve my... anyone if we did," Macron said with a low groan as he slowly stretched out his legs.

"Put him with the others until I decide what to do with them," Mandra instructed to Bale.

"Yes, sir," Bale replied.

He wrapped his arm around Ariel and guided her to the exit. She worriedly looked over his shoulder. He chuckled and kissed her temple.

"We'll safely release all of them," he promised.

She kissed him and smiled. "I know. I'm just a worrywart about having a bunch of Tasier-loving dragons releasing them," she confessed.

He threw his head back and laughed, then lifted her off her feet. Several warriors grinned with amusement as they passed by.

"Trust me when I say there isn't a dragon on any ship who would harm one of your precious animals with you around. Besides, after the last incident with those damn creatures, I think the little furballs have lost their appeal," he said.

Lucky me, he thought, thinking of all the trouble the furry creatures had caused.

Lucky us, his dragon purred, thinking how happy his mate would be when the tiny creatures were safely released.

∾

Minor Moon of Leviathan

. . .

Arosa was lying in Tamblin's arms with her head on his shoulder when a familiar presence drew her attention to the entrance of the cave. She brushed her fingers tenderly along Tamblin's relaxed face. He was sleeping deeply—a combination of their lovemaking and his exhaustion from the last few months of conflict.

She faded, reforming next to the bed. A gown appeared around her, and she glided across the cave to the entrance. A smile brightened her face when she saw Arilla waving her arms like a conductor in front of an orchestra. Beyond, the burnt ground transformed as a light rain fell. Colorful mushrooms pushed up through the ground to carpet the once scorched landscape.

Thank you, sister, Arosa said as she floated over to her.

"You're welcome," Arilla replied with a grin.

"Where have you been?" she asked.

Arilla shrugged. "Exploring, checking in on old friends, giving my sister time to find out where her heart truly belongs," she stated.

"I didn't realize we could have a heart—until now," she replied.

Arilla smiled in response. They stood side-by-side, gazing out at the world. Arosa watched as dozens of transports arrived on the planet. A swift search of the vessels reassured her it was only the Valdier returning the confiscated Tasiers to the moon.

"What will happen next, Arilla? I love him. I can't imagine existing without him," she said.

"You'll be happy," Arilla responded, threading her arm through Arosa's.

"Aikaterina—" she began in a hushed tone.

Arilla laughed and squeezed her arm. "I don't think you need to worry about Aikaterina. She has her own challenges to deal with, thanks to us," she retorted in a reassuring tone.

Arosa looked at her sister. "What will you do?" she asked.

Arilla wiggled her nose. "I'll explore more worlds, visit my sister occasionally, help the Dragonlings get into mischief, and try to stay one step ahead of the Elders," she said.

"It sounds like you are on a mission," she reflected.

Arilla laughed. "Yes, I guess I am. What do you think?" she asked, waving a hand at her handiwork.

Arosa gazed out at the healed landscape and smiled. "Beautiful, just like you," she teased.

"I'll miss you, Arosa," Arilla confessed.

"I'll miss you, too, sister," she said.

She trailed her fingers along Arilla's arm as she slowly vanished. A smile of contentment curved her lips. She wondered if the universe was ready for a renegade Goddess on a mission. The thought caused her to laugh.

"What's so funny?" Tamblin asked, sliding his arms around her waist and pulling her back against him.

"I thought you would still be asleep," she teased.

He kissed her neck. "I missed you. You've been busy," he said.

"A gift from my sister Arilla," she confessed.

"Will you stay with me?" he quietly inquired.

She heard the note of uncertainty in his voice. She turned in his arms and caressed his cheek. He gazed at her with a look that laid bare his soul. The love shining in his eyes took her breath away and made her want to cry—in a good way.

"I love you, Tamblin. My heart belongs to you," she said, grasping his hand and pressing it against her chest.

"You will always be my Arosa. The beautiful Queen of the Wood Fairies who captured my heart," he murmured before capturing her lips in a passionate kiss.

Valdier:

Several months later

"So tells me what's the matters," Morah Reykill said, adjusting her golden glasses.

"I've met a man—a human—and I'm not sure what to do. One minute I want to feel his touch, and the next, I'm seriously considering burying him up to his neck in the ground," Arilla confessed, lying back against the pillows on Morah's bed.

Morah tapped on the tablet she was holding and looked over the rim of her glasses. "You's comes to the right person for advice," she calmly said.

Note from the author:

I hope you enjoyed Tamblin and Arosa's story. The characters from the Kingdom of Glitter and Sandora captured my imagination when I first wrote about them in *Ambushing Ariel*. After writing *For the Love of Tia* and *The Dragonlings and the Magic Four-Leaf Clover*, I knew I would have to write Tamblin and Arosa's story. Yet, as you can imagine, I've also fallen in love with the mysterious, powerful, and charming 'Goddesses'. Arosa and Arilla captured my heart the moment they first appeared in my series. So, as much as this will probably get me in a lot of trouble, there will be more stories from the Dragon Lords, the Dragonlings, and yes—there will even be one for a **Renegade Goddess**.

PS: Don't forget to look for Easter Eggs to some of my other series!!

And if you're craving another PG-13 romantic adventure, one of my favorites is: **First Awakenings:**

Lieutenant Commander Ashton "Ash" Haze has gotten into some outrageous situations following his best friend, but this one really takes the cake. Ash is in a whole other galaxy now, separated from his team—who could have landed anywhere—and well, it's sure to be an adventure!

Kella Ta'Qui is a Turbinta, a member of a guild who discard their genetic identities in favor of what they train to become: assassins. Her first mission is to kill whatever was inside the unusual capsule that landed on Tesla Terra, but predator becomes prey when she is wounded by her target. She stumbles into a group who plan to sell her to the highest bidder—and her target rescues her.

Ash and Kella's alliance is like none this galaxy has ever seen! But will it lead to happy ending?

With endearing characters, daring escapes, nail-biting battles, and love found in the most unlikely of places, I hope you'll like this book as much as I do!

~Susan

ADDITIONAL STORIES

If you loved this story by me (S.E. Smith) please leave a review!

You can discover additional books at http://sesmithya.com. There you can also sign up for my newsletter to hear about my latest releases!

Find your favorite way to keep in touch below:

Newsletter direct link: http://eepurl.com/bBgI6v

RSS Feed: http://feeds.feedburner.com/MyFeedName

Facebook: https://facebook.com/YABooksSESmith

Twitter: https://twitter.com/SESmithYA

Pinterest: https://www.pinterest.com/SESmithYA/

Youtube: https://goo.gl/AjsvBt

Tumblr: http://sesmithya.tumblr.com/

Instagram: https://instagram.com/sesmithya/

Epic Science Fiction / Action Adventure

Project Gliese 581G Series

An international team leave Earth to investigate a mysterious object in our solar system that was clearly made by someone, someone who isn't from Earth. Discover new worlds and conflicts in a sci-fi adventure sure to become your favorite!

First Awakenings

Survivor Skills

New Adult / Young Adult

Breaking Free Series

Makayla steals her grandfather's sailboat and embarks on a journey that will challenge everything she has ever believed about herself.

Voyage of the Defiance

Capture of the Defiance

Makayla is older now, but when she needs help, her friends from years ago join new and unexpected allies. Capture of the Defiance is a thriller mystery that stands on its own as danger reveals itself in sudden, heart-stopping moments.

The Dust Series

Fragments of a comet hit Earth, and Dust wakes to discover the world as he knew it is gone. It isn't the only thing that has changed, though, so has Dust…

Dust: Before and After (Book 1)

Dust: A New World Order (Book 2)

Dragonlings of Valdier

The Valdier, Sarafin, and Curizan Lords had children who just cannot stop getting into trouble! There is nothing as cute or funny as magical, shapeshifting kids, and nothing as heartwarming as family.

The Dragonlings and the Magic Four-Leaf Clover

ABOUT THE AUTHOR

S.E. Smith is an *internationally acclaimed, New York Times* **and** *USA TODAY Bestselling* author of science fiction, romance, fantasy, paranormal, and contemporary works for adults, young adults, and children. She enjoys writing a wide variety of genres that pull her readers into worlds that take them away.

www.ingramcontent.com/pod-product-compliance
Lightning Source LLC
Chambersburg PA
CBHW051652260626
47170CB00004B/1457